Jane McLoughlin

AT YELLOW LAKE

F
FRANCES LINCOLN
CHILDREN'S BOOKS

Chapter One

—

ETTA

The way the old lady looked at Mom and me, it was like we were buying Buckingham Palace from her, not a 1992-model Regency Northland mobile home.

Snooty wasn't the word. Her red-smeared lips kept tightening up and her eyes twitched like she was scared of something. A disease, maybe, or invisible germs that might seep out from our trailer trash breath and settle like toxic dew on her white vinyl sofa and chairs.

'Now this here's the master bedroom.' The old lady's butt wobbled as she tiptoed down the narrow hallway. She wasn't fat, but underneath her thin polyester shorts, her skin hung down like lumpy oatmeal off a wooden spoon.

'The *master* bedroom,' Mom echoed, raising an eyebrow the way she did when she was making a joke that was for just the two of us. 'Sounds like my mother,' she rasped, poking me in the ribs with her elbow in case I'd gone deaf. 'Don't she sound just like the Duchess?'

The Duchess didn't live in a trailer park, though. The Duchess had a five-bedroom home with a two-acre lawn and a driveway longer than all the trailers in the North Country Mobile Home Community lined up end to end. Unlike Mom, the Duchess had married somebody decent – my Grandpa Vernon, who gave her anything she wanted, who stuck by her through thick and thin, who'd stick with anybody he loved, no matter what.

The way he stuck with Mom, and Jesse, Cole and me. His only daughter and his only grandkids, who were all named after outlaws because our father had liked imagining he was a genuine gangster, and not just a low life who held up liquor stores with hunting knives or sawn-off shotguns.

It was Grandpa's money that was letting us buy the old lady's trailer. (I couldn't stop calling it that. I was supposed to say, 'mobile home', or even better, '*manufactured* home', like the old lady did.) Just like it was Grandpa's money that kept us all together when Mom and my *real* dad split up, when Mom and my *step*dad split up, when Mom took up with that guy who was running a call girl ring from his apartment. This time round, Grandpa's money was helping us escape from Mom's latest crappy boyfriend and move all the way up to northern Wisconsin.

The old lady's trailer didn't seem so bad, not as bad as the ones that we could actually afford. Most of them were like crack dens on wheels, with mildewed walls and tattered sheets hanging in the windows. This trailer didn't smell of pee or have burn marks on the carpet. Still, the old lady's knick-knack addiction made it hard to judge. The bedroom walls were plastered with faded pictures of her grandkids and of pets that had probably been put down years ago. She had miniature glass farm animals on her bedside table: pigs and piglets, cows with their calves, a headless rooster. On her chest of drawers there were ceramic plates commemorating the lives of famous dead people, as though Elvis Presley and Princess Diana were part of her family too.

The tiny bathroom was even worse. The vanity was cluttered up with Avon bath figurines, and there were scented candles shaped like animals perched along the sides of the tub. Mom eyeballed them all like she was looking for something nasty hidden underneath. I caught a glimpse of the two of us in the old lady's mirror: both with long hair, frayed jeans, faded T-shirts. If I crossed my eyes a little to make things blurry, we could be identical twins. She still wore a size four, same as me. The only things that made her look thirty-nine and not fourteen like me were the lines on her face, the stains on her teeth and the color of her hair. Hers was dyed blonde. Mine was no color at all.

Mom found what she wanted. As soon the old lady came in, she started tutting and shaking her head. The old lady panicked and tried to smile – she knew something was up.

'I forgot to offer you ladies some coffee,' she said, her voice all sweet, like we were her friends, like we were company now. 'Maybe you'd care to come and take another look at the kitchen?'

'That's OK,' Mom said, as she peeked behind the shower curtain like a detective on TV. 'I think we've seen just about enough.' She looked at the old lady as though she felt sorry for her. 'That mold around the bath mat.' Mom held out her hands and shrugged, shaking her head as if it was breaking her heart to let the old lady down.

Months later, I'd remember that lady, and how her lip trembled when Mom pointed out the mold and

4

said that maybe the asking price – $40,000 – was a little bit steep for a damp-ridden used trailer. It was too much for her, being humiliated by people who were so far beneath her, but had somehow found a way to get the upper hand.

It's weird, that. If Mom hadn't noticed the mold and made such a big fuss about it, we wouldn't have moved, because we wouldn't have been able to afford the trailer. We would've stayed where we were, in Minnesota. So the good things that happened at Yellow Lake would never have happened. And the bad things? Who knows. Some things just can't be stopped. Some things can't be fixed by running away, like me and my mom were about to do.

PETER

Under a gray sky that seemed heavy enough to crush him, Peter watched his mother's coffin being lowered into the Sussex soil. A priest was droning words he couldn't understand and a top-hat-wearing undertaker handed him a tray of clumpy dirt. What was he supposed to do with it? Take it home? Put it in his pockets as some sick souvenir? Finally, the top-hat man nodded towards the hole in the ground. Peter picked up a handful of soil and dropped it in. The sound it made on the wooden box was like dry rain.

This was wrong. This was all wrong.

He stepped back from the hole. What the hell was he doing, helping them cover her up? He should be climbing into the ground, scraping off the dirt, lifting her out, carrying her back home.

He felt a hand on his shoulder and shrugged it off. Why wouldn't people just leave him alone? Did they think he wanted their pity? Did they think *she* wanted their pathetic sniveling?

His father was the worst. After it was over, and the priest had gone back to his church, and the undertakers were waiting outside the big black car that would take them back for sandwiches and tea, he lingered at the graveside – the lonely widowed husband. Peter watched from the back seat of the limo, hating every bob of his father's head – up and down, up and down – and the way he made it look like he was sobbing, made it seem as though he were grieving, as though he actually cared. Peter knew what he was *really* thinking: how he'd done everything right on the day, how he'd handled the funeral with such skill, such care, such amazing style.

Peter was struggling to keep awake, trying not to let the car's heat and the day's emotion send him to sleep. He needed to stay alert. He needed to be ready – for what, he wasn't sure, but he'd been praying all day for an omen or a sign. It didn't have to be anything major, he told whoever he was praying to, just a hint about what he could do to make things right again.

And then, just as he was about to nod off, he saw something through the car window. It wasn't much of a vision, and it was very far away. A tiny gap in the clouds opened up, letting a bright shaft of sunlight shine across the downlands and flicker on the distant sea. The flash of blue water jolted him awake and, in a moment that was perfect and clear, Peter *remembered*.

Yellow Lake.

JONAH

Somewhere in the distance, a white man was mowing his lawn.

Jonah lay sprawled on the forest floor and imagined that the sound was something else – a crow, droning and circling overhead, high above the oak and aspen trees, swooping out over the lake; a hungry wolf cub, crying for its mother; the shrill, clean whistle of a ceremonial flute.

It was just a lawnmower, though, and it reminded him of the list he'd found on the kitchen table the day he left Minneapolis.

Sweep out our half of the garage. Mow the strip of grass by the road. Go to the laundromat, for God's sake – your clothes are starting to stink! Pick up some milk. XX Mom

Thinking of his mother – even her whiny voice when she nagged him about chores – was a mistake.

He couldn't start missing her. Not now. He was sixteen years old – a man, not a baby. He had to do manly things. Hunt animals. Fish with a spear. Build shelters.

The instructions he'd read online for making the wigwam said that building shelters had been women's work. Was that why it was all going wrong?

It had started well enough. By the end of his first day in the woods he'd already cleared the ground of scrub and rotten leaves. He'd marked out his circle using the string he bought at the Hardware Hank in Welmer, the nearest town. He'd gathered up the long thin saplings that the shelter's plans had called for. That was when it got complicated. The saplings had to be bent first, so Jonah stood on one end and grabbed the other with his hands. But the stupid things kept springing out from under his feet, making him lose his balance and crash onto the ground.

Lying on his back, looking up at the blue patch between the green canopy of oak and elm leaves, he felt like he was being watched. Something, or someone, was laughing at his pathetic efforts. Was it a trickster, punishing him for doing women's work?

'It isn't my fault,' he wanted to shout. 'I don't have a woman to help me. What else can I do? If you want me to be a real man, send me a woman.'

The mid-afternoon heat was taking its toll, even in the shady woods. It wasn't just the wigwam that was wearing him down. He was thirsty, and he was almost out of water. That meant another three-mile hike into Welmer and the chance of some nosy local noticing him and wondering what he was up to. Further north there were tribal communities, so a dark-skinned kid wouldn't attract suspicion. But around here, Jonah wasn't sure. Somebody might stop him, ask questions – or worse.

He stood up and slipped through a gap in the trees. He pushed aside the line of saplings that kept the white man's world safely at bay.

There was always the cabin.

A hundred or so yards from where he'd made his camp was a small house, somebody's second home, one of the dozen or so that were dotted along the Yellow Lake shoreline. It looked older than the other ones Jonah had seen. Its paint was peeling, but only enough to see that its walls were made of real wood, not aluminum siding. It was a solid house, hand-built, board by board, by real human beings, using saws and nails and hammers. It was a white man's house, but it seemed to

Jonah like it belonged in the woods, as if being surrounded by so much beautiful land had given it a soul.

There'd be water inside too. Maybe going in and turning on the faucet wouldn't be the right thing to do, but it would be the easiest, wouldn't it? He could give the door a little push, see what happened.

No. Even the thought of it made his cheeks burn. What was the matter with him? Is that why he'd come to Yellow Lake – to take the easy way? He stepped backwards, through the undergrowth, and crept back to his camp.

He found his water bottle and gulped down the last delicious drops. That was enough for now. And tomorrow? He'd think of something, find a way. He tucked the bottle into his backpack and sat down. He closed his eyes and listened.

Chipmunks scurried over dry leaves. Birds hooted and flapped their wings. Acorns dropped onto the ground and, at the bottom of the hill, the lake lapped the shore like a gentle heartbeat.

The spirits of the forest were speaking to him, as he knew they would.

He just had to listen – they'd show him the way.

Chapter Two
ETTA

Moving day was hot and humid. Breathing was like struggling against a wet pillow. Everything moved in slow motion. Even the flies and June bugs buzzed in a lower gear.

Grandpa Vernon came along to help us load up the van. Mom was quiet, the way she always was around him. What was it – shame? Guilt? She found a spot of shade under a spindly tree, while Jesse and Cole heaved the last of the boxes into the back and piled the sheets and bedding high in the seats, blocking out any view from the rear window. She sucked on a cigarette, hunching down, glancing around like a teenager about to get caught. Grandpa stood next to her, quiet. At times like this, his brown eyes seemed to get bigger, making him look like a dog that'd been kicked but couldn't understand why. He whispered something to Mom that must have really pissed her off, because she flung her cigarette onto the dusty ground, stomped on it, and waved her arms hysterically, shouting, 'I said, *no*, I meant *no*, now will you just let me *go*, please.' She ran into the apartment building and slammed the door.

Jesse and Cole got into the van. Jesse lit up a cigarette, Cole popped open a can of beer. They were grown men now, nineteen and twenty, more like my uncles than my brothers. Grandpa Vernon looked lonesome under that scrubby tree so I walked over to him and we watched Jesse and Cole horse around the way they did when they were kids, honking the horn, playing with the steering wheel.

'Come back with me, Ettie,' Grandpa said after a while. He sounded like Scarecrow in *The Wizard of Oz*, trying to convince Dorothy not to go back to Kansas. 'You can stay with us until you graduate and then we can fix you up for college.'

I put my arm around him, touching the loose skin around his middle, where he'd lost weight after the operation. I could feel a pointed bone, his bottom rib.

'I know what your mom thinks,' Grandpa said, 'but she never sees things straight.'

Right on cue, as if she'd heard what he was saying,

Mom came outside, all calm, collected, businesslike – the boss.

'That's it, now, Etta. Get in the van.'

She was standing with Mrs Jansen, the apartment manager, who handed her an envelope in exchange for the keys. She shook Mrs Jansen's hand, like they were both high-flying businesswomen who'd just sealed an amazing deal. Never mind that Mom was wearing short, red cut-offs and a Hooters T-shirt, or that Mrs Jansen had half a ladle of gravy spilled down the front of her polyester waitress top.

I never got the chance to say anything to Grandpa, not even a, 'Thanks for trying.' But he knew I couldn't stay, that I couldn't leave Mom on her own. I had to take care of her. He didn't like it, but I think he understood.

'Don't let her see this.' He slipped me a couple of twenties. 'Don't let her take it.'

Then he walked over to where the van was parked and Mom was in the driver's seat, yelling at Cole for having his feet up on the dashboard. He dipped his hand into his wallet again, and did the same for Mom, only for her it was fifties.

'We both love you, Susie. You need anything, you just ask.'

Mom leaned out and gave him a peck on the cheek. For a split second it seemed like she was going to say something else, or lean against Grandpa and sob into his chest. But she just smiled at him, rolled up the window, and drove away without even waving.

The trip up north took most of the day. The solid maple and ash trees of southern Minnesota gave way to pine trees and skinny silver birches. The soil went from dark brown to sandy red. The sky was cloudless, but the blue in Wisconsin seemed duller and washed out, like faded denim. Businesses changed from seedcorn dealerships to gun shops. Bright Day-Glo signs shouted out, Guns-Bait-Ammo. The roads got bumpier too, and all along the gravel shoulder there were dead animals – deer mostly, all ages and sizes, but also smaller animals, like racoons and foxes. We couldn't have traveled far, 300 miles or so, but Welmer seemed a lifetime away from Minnesota, and in another country altogether, not just another state.

It was almost dark when we got to the 'community'. The trailer park was on the outskirts of town, next to a hiking trail that had once been the railroad tracks. But, as hard as it was to admit, the North Pines Community wasn't such a bad place. The grass in the lots was, well, greener, than most of the brown, patchy lawns we'd passed by. The roads and sidewalks were smooth and shiny under the street lights. The trailers actually looked like the 'homes' they were meant to be. Some of them had shutters and gables, others had solid cedar decks. Ours was the only trailer that looked like an old-fashioned mobile home, but even ours was clean and kept up.

Inside was just as nice – once the old lady with the wobbly butt had taken down her knick-knacks, we realized – no crappy paneling, no chintz. The walls were clean, the tiles were real. The bathroom looked brand new.

'Jeez, it's just like a hotel,' Jesse whooped as he lumbered into the kitchen. To celebrate he chucked an empty beer can onto the black marble counter and Mom whisked it away before he could even reach into the cooler for another one.

'Watch it,' she said. 'This is our home now. We're gonna keep it clean.'

And so we did, at least for the first few days. Mom was like a kid on vacation, skipping around the place, up at the crack of dawn polishing the sink, sweeping the kitchen floor, marvelling at how easily the dirt came off the terracotta tiles.

Then, one morning, somebody turned up – a guy, of course.

'Hey!' A big booming voice vibrated deep in his chest. He rattled the front door, his smile gleaming through the screen. That made a change for Mom – decent teeth.

He had a decent car, too – a metallic, blue Beemer that looked brand new. And he was young, for Mom, anyway. His hair was tied back in a tight ponytail and he had a scraggly beard, like a biker's.

Mom rushed through from the bedroom to meet him, eyes wide, mouth open. Was this a good surprise or a bad surprise? Either way, the man let out a huge whoop and picked her up in his arms like she was a tiny child. He swung her around, bashing her legs on the kitchen counter.

'Careful now,' she squeaked. 'Those units are new.'

He put her down and pinched her on the butt. Then he came into the living room where I was watching TV. He raised his eyebrows.

'I'm Kyle,' he said, baring his teeth. 'You must be the little girl.'

'Etta,' I said. 'My name's Etta.'

'You be nice now,' Mom said, before he grabbed

her by the waist and gave her another twirl.

It wasn't long before Kyle turned into a 'regular'. That's what Mom called her boyfriends after she'd been going out with them for a couple weeks.

'Regulars.' Jeez. What did that sound like?

PETER

It was dawn, and he'd have to leave for the train station in a few minutes. He looked around his room for anything left behind. The door of the oak closet was open and the empty hangers hung from the rail like dried shoulder bones. The floral wallpaper was covered with fraying, faded posters of bands he used to like – Blink 182, Funeral for a Friend, My Chemical Romance. The faces staring out at him looked pathetic now, all that made-up anger and poser alienation.

He did a final check of his carry-on luggage – passport, boarding pass, his dad's credit card, map. He looked into his holdall one more time before closing it. Carefully slipping his hand into the inner pocket, he felt the velvet cloth which held the lock of his mother's hair, remembering the day he'd cut it from her head.

'I'm not doing it,' he'd whined. He'd tried to look at Mum, really see her, gaze right into her eyes, but the room in the hospice had been too bright. It was unnatural, all that light. It made everything too clear.

'It's my hair or it's toenail clippings. Your choice.'

She'd handed him a pair of nail scissors, and lowered her head so that he could reach. A tiny patch of hair had managed to cling to her head during the chemotherapy storm that had yanked all the other clumps out by their roots. He cut a wispy lock that, nestled in his palm, looked like a baby's. With bony, translucent fingers, his mother wrapped it in a tissue.

'Take this to the lake.'

He couldn't answer. If he said anything, it would be like admitting that she was going to die.

'You heard me, didn't you?'

He nodded. She motioned for him to get closer, to sit on the bed and rest his head on her fragile shoulders. For a moment, they sat that way, Mum touching his spiky hair with her fingertips, Peter looking out of the window at the cars in the car park, willing himself not to cry.

'I don't want to die here,' she said, sighing. A simple statement, as if it were no big deal. 'I thought I'd have enough time to go back.'

Outside the window, a florist's van pulled up,

blocking Peter's view. He looked at the floor, counting out the brown and beige tiles, one to ten, one to ten, over and over, saying the numbers in his head, trying to block out what his mother was saying about dying, about funerals, about what he should wear.

'Petey? Honey?'

She must have been waiting for him to answer, but he had nothing to say. He was empty, pathetic – a useless, crap son.

'You'll do that for me, won't you? When this is over?'

She picked up the tissue packet and handed it to him. She smiled, like she always did. A joke for the two of them.

'You'll take me to Yellow Lake and bury me in the sand?'

The wolfed-down breakfast was a mistake. His Weetabix and milk tasted like damp sawdust. Just thinking about what he was going to do made his mouth dry up and his stomach turn. He was always sick when he was nervous. He'd have to stay near a toilet.

He rinsed his bowl, pouring the last of the milk down the sink, and took his passport out again. How carefully would they check it? He looked about ten years old in the picture, his eyes peeking out from stupid, too-long bangs. But he was taller now, nearly the height of his father. Surely he could pass for sixteen. And anyway, the airline people wouldn't be worrying about his age, would they? Wouldn't they be too busy searching him for dodgy chemicals or devices concealed inside his sneakers? He'd be whisked through security, just another white English kid. It would be simple. He would fly to America, do what he had to do, then get back before anybody even had time to raise the alarm.

After Mum died, his father had only taken a week off work – business as usual. His father didn't use that expression. Even *he* wasn't cold enough to use language like that, but that was the impression he gave the world. Just get on with it – that was his motto. Just get on with it, as if nothing had happened.

Then, one night, Dad announced that he was going to Italy, on his own. He'd be gone a week, spending a few days each in Mum's favorite places – the Amalfi Coast, Rome, Venice, Milan. It would give him a chance to heal, he said, a chance to see the world he and Mum had shared with new eyes – alone.

Bollocks, Peter thought. A nice holiday away from me, more like, catching a few rays, spending Mum's life insurance money on five-star hotels and pool-side cocktails.

It didn't take long for Peter to realize that his father was doing him a favor. This was his big chance – with Dad out of the way, he'd be able to fly to America, all by himself. For weeks he'd been too excited to sleep, planning his mission, working things out in his head. He could stay with his uncle in Minneapolis, make up some story, string him along. From there, it'd be easy to get to Yellow Lake. They had trains in America, didn't they? They had buses?

And now, despite his pounding heart and heaving stomach, he was ready. He closed the front door, slipped through the side gate, ducked behind a hedge as he passed the neighbors' house. Epsom Road was empty this early in the morning, silent except for the hum of a milk float a few streets away. He should have felt lonely, but he wasn't alone. Mum was traveling with him – a tiny part of her, anyway, just the way she had wanted.

JONAH

Night came. The forest floor was teeming with life. Jonah turned over on the ground, imagining fist-sized spiders, hard-shelled beetles with pincers as big as his fingers. He thought about the spirits watching over him, but even that didn't calm him down – the crunching, rustling sounds filled his mind with terror. He sat up on the beach towel he'd brought to sleep on. He wrapped himself in a thin cotton sheet, but it was no use against the onslaught of insects that were bombarding his face, flying into his nose, hovering around his ears like drones.

He got up, dropping the sheet, shaking the imaginary bugs off his clothes. He had to get out of here – *now*, before he went crazy, before he was eaten alive.

The cabin – that was the place to go. There'd be beds inside, with warm, soft blankets on them. There'd be screens on the window to keep out the mosquitoes and gnats. There'd be water too. Didn't he *need* that? Didn't everybody need fresh water to live?

He stepped through the trees, tiptoed along the narrow path that cut through the woods. He stopped when he got to the cabin's front door. He looked around, as if somebody were watching. What he was about to do was wrong – he knew that – not just a seriously uncool thing to do, but an actual crime. Breaking and entering.

Never mind, he thought. Just do it.

Forcing the cabin's lock didn't take much effort. A few strong nudges with his hip and shoulder and the door flew open and bashed against the wall. He took a lighter from the pocket of his jeans and fired it up. Inside the door there was a list of instructions on how to turn everything on – electricity, water pump, gas for the furnace in winter.

So much for being at one with the forest, he thought.

He walked through the cabin, feeling his way along the walls, through the doorways, until he found a bedroom. He tumbled into a bed – warm and soft, just like he'd imagined – and pulled up the covers.

He woke up at sunrise, and opened the curtains beside the bed. Through the window, he could see sunlight dancing on the lake below, making the tips of the waves sparkle like dazzling yellow jewels.

His stomach did a flip, but he knew it wasn't hunger – it was more like disgust. What was he doing, anyway, hiding out in a place like this? He was Ojibwe, one of the original people, the *Anishinaabe*. He shouldn't need beds, he shouldn't need bathrooms – he shouldn't need anything more than his hands, a knife, the forest's bounty.

He got up and made the bed, smoothing out any sign that he'd been there. In the bathroom he washed his face with the last spits of water that were still in the faucet. He looked in the mirror, pulled back his hair – long enough now to tie it back if he wanted.

That sick feeling came back while he wiped the sink with a lacy pink hand towel – still the white man, he thought, worried about keeping things clean. He'd wanted to turn his back on everything that kept him from his true path and he'd failed miserably at the first minor hitch. He might as well go straight back to Minneapolis and start the summer job his mother had lined up for him at Walmart.

In the kitchen he found the instructions for

turning on the water, and filled up an empty milk jug. He looked at the phone that was hanging on the pine-paneled wall. He picked it up, heard a dial tone. Maybe he should call his mother. What was she thinking, now that he was gone? Did she miss him? He'd left a note, explaining what he intended to do – find a place where he could be true to his heritage, live the Ojibwe way – but even when he was writing it, he imagined her reaction. Coming home from work, climbing the stairs to their apartment, heaving the grocery bags onto the kitchen table, shouting his name. He taped the note to the fridge, knowing that she'd look there. She probably laughed when she read it, just like she laughed when she talked to her friends about him on the phone.

'Oh, yeah, he's going through this *Indian* phase.' Pause. Listen. 'Ha ha ha. I suppose it could be worse – neo-Nazis or country music. Ha ha ha.'

Jonah put the phone down. If she was worried, well, that was OK by him. How did she dare call it a phase? Maybe *she'd* turned her back on her own heritage, maybe *she* was ashamed of what she was, but that didn't give her the right to mock him. How did she dare, when the Ojibwe blood that flowed through his veins came from her?

His hands shaking with anger, he took the water jug and went outside. He locked the cabin door and strode back up to the woods. The sky had clouded over. It was starting to rain, but Jonah didn't care. He heard his mother's voice in his head, 'You? An Indian? Give me a break!'

Bits of the wigwam were still on the ground where he'd left them – the rope, the twigs, the birch bark. All he had to do was put them together. He picked up a slender branch, ran his fingers along the smooth surface. He bent it, holding each end tightly in his hands. He felt the spirits of the forest – watching this time, seeing what he was up to. He heard the voice – 'Hiding in a cabin because you got scared of some bugs' – only this time she whispered.

He took a deep breath, shook his shoulders and arms to loosen his muscles. He heard the birds, the breeze, the swoosh of distant waves. He picked up another branch, bent it, placed it on the ground. And another one, and another one.

When he was finished, he stood up, smiling. The saplings stayed bent. His mother's voice had shut up.

Chapter Three
—
ETTA

The good, safe feeling we took with us to Welmer lasted about a month. So did the heat. I spent most of my time watching daytime TV, praying the clanking air conditioner wouldn't conk out. Sometimes I'd walk around Welmer. Ah, Welmer – a drugstore, two taverns and a Hardware Hank.

There were other things, too. Gangs of high school boys practiced football on the school athletics field beside the trailer park. Whenever I went outside, even if it was to put some wet laundry on the clothesline, they'd watch me. They wouldn't shout or whistle, but I could feel them staring. What was it, the way I looked? Average height, average weight, average bra size – nothing out of the ordinary, just a fourteen-year-old girl with dust-colored hair.

Mom got a job as a housekeeper at the Northern Pines Hotel and Suites, on the outskirts of town, towards the lakes that were dotted around the county. It was a decent place, even if the pay was lousy. She was good at her job, especially on days when her back wasn't playing up, so her hourly pay, with tips, was enough to keep us going, as long as neither of us got sick. Some weekends we drove to Duluth, spent her money on clothes and shoes, had lunch on the way, or a picnic on the lake.

Lake Superior was like an ocean – no sign of land on the other side, just an endless expanse of steely-gray blue. The first time we saw it, Mom pulled the van into a roadside picnic area. Before we could even unpack our lunch, she hopped out of the van and raced down to the shore. She seemed so happy and excited I thought she was going to do cartwheels across the scrubby sand. But by the time I got the picnic things together and clambered out to join her, she was slumped down on the water's edge with her face in her hands, sobbing uncontrollably.

'What is it? Mom? What's the matter?'

She carried on like that, crying and shaking her head, so I left her alone. The beach was deserted. It was a cloudy day, and the wind felt cold, even though it was summer. The sky seemed bigger here than in Welmer. And the lake? It made me feel tiny. I knew I wasn't alone, because I could hear Mom sniffling and snuffling a few yards away, but I could've been the only person on a planet covered entirely with water.

I never found out what Mom was crying about. I've got some ideas now, but at the time I thought maybe she'd been to the same park before, maybe with the Duchess when she was little. Or else maybe she felt frightened, like me, of so much water and space. After a few minutes, I heard the hiss of her lighter and smelled the smoke from her cigarette. We got into the van after she stubbed out her butt, and went shopping like nothing had happened.

At the Northern Pine Lodge and Suites she got to use their pool and spa, and some days she'd sneak me in the back way. We'd have a sauna, and then a quick dip in the pool. It was nice, then, like being on vacation, just the two of us.

She was different when there were no men around, when it was just her and me. She was calmer, her face looked softer, prettier without all the make-up. She was smarter, too – lots smarter. One afternoon in the sauna, stretching herself out on the hot wooden bench, she closed her eyes and sighed.

'You know what, Et? I think I might go back to college.'

'College?'

'Yeah. College. Why do you sound so shocked?' she laughed. 'I finished a whole semester before I had Jesse.'

Before she could say any more, a man with a hairy beer belly came in, poured some water on the coals, slapped his sweaty butt down on the bench across from me. Mom didn't move. She acted like she didn't even realize he was there, but she changed. You couldn't tell, unless you knew what to look for. The way her lip pouted out. The way her voice got sharper.

'English Lit, that was my major. Shakespeare. Jane Austen. I was a real bookworm in my day. There was nothing I liked more than reading.' She smiled at me, glancing at the fat guy like a wise-ass kid. 'Except partying, I guess, and pissing off my parents.' She thought that was really funny, at least she pretended she did. 'And getting myself knocked up all the time.'

This made her laugh so hard she started to cough. She sat up, looked at the hairy fat man, and coughed even louder. I don't know if it was because the man was so hairy or because he'd heard what she said, but she laughed and coughed so much I thought she'd wet her bikini bottoms.

It was always like that. It didn't matter if she liked him or not, or even if she knew him or not – whenever a man came into the picture it would wreck things for us.

Like Kyle was about to do.

It took me a while to realize that Kyle was no accident. I felt stupid about that later. Of course he was the reason we moved to Welmer. Why else would she have packed us off to such an out of the way place? Of course Mom had known him for a long time – her version of a long time, anyway. He must have latched onto her back in Minnesota, when she was a waitress, or met her at some bar when she was out with her previous boyfriend.

Cole and Jesse didn't hang around for long – Jesse had to train with his Air Force reserves unit and Cole missed the girlfriend he'd left behind. So, it was just Mom and me.

And Kyle.

At first I didn't see much of him. He'd come by on Friday nights. Mom would drag herself back from her longest shift of the week and hop in the shower, scrub off the sweat and grime. She'd put on clean shorts and a cute top, do her hair up, slap on some make-up. Only they'd never go out – they'd just stay in, watching TV.

She got touchy when I asked her about it. 'He brings the pizza, don't he? He buys the beer. Ain't that better than nothing?'

Sometimes he'd come early, before she was ready. He'd sneak up the steps, open the door so quick that before you knew it, there he was – sprawled out on the couch, feet on the coffee table, like it was his place, like he was the boss.

He didn't bother me, though. He just watched TV. And like I said, Mom seemed ten years younger when she was with him, so I tried to give him the benefit of the doubt. He seemed relatively normal. Maybe I could relax for a change.

We had a good month, Mom and me – nearly all of August.

And then it happened.

PETER

Before he got to the station, Peter was sick – twice. The first time he brought up the Weetabix. The second time, nothing, just thin, orange liquid. It was the same when he got to the airport. Inside the terminal, he rushed into the toilets and heaved so loudly that a cleaner knocked on the door.

'You right in there, mister? You need help?'

Peter opened the door so the man wouldn't think he was a druggy who'd taken an overdose. He shook his head, teeth chattering, body trembling, eyes watering.

When he got to the check-in counter, a bored woman questioned him about his luggage. 'Yes, no.' He knew the drill. Then she put his passport into a scanning machine. She watched the screen, blinked once, gave it back. That was it. No panic, no alarms, no flashing lights.

At security, the story was the same – a scan, a

glance, a nod through to the other side. No one seemed startled by the rumbles and growls that were coming from inside him. No one looked scared of the pale, zombie face he'd seen in the toilet mirror while he rinsed out his mouth.

Finally, he stepped onto the plane and took his seat next to the window. The man beside him nodded and grunted as he squeezed past, then retreated into his newspaper. The relief – the feeling that he was actually on his way – was almost overwhelming. Peter took in deep breaths, laughing to himself as the threat of tears stung his face. Bloody hell. Wouldn't that be just like something he'd do? Start crying when he'd nearly made it? Cause a fuss, arouse suspicion, get chucked off the plane?

Minutes later, though, he was flying through the air. He watched the cars, the rooftops, the streets of London fade, then disappear. The 747's engines shook his insides. Finally, it was happening. *He'd done it*. He looked out of the window at the green fields and rolling hills far below him. When the plane slipped into a mountain of gray and white cloud, the England he'd always known vanished completely.

JONAH

It rained all day, in sharp, heavy spits, like a spray of tiny knives. High in the trees, a cluster of crows was squawking. It was as if his mother were up there, cackling out ridicule, waiting for him to give up and accept defeat. Well, he wouldn't.

Gradually, the wigwam took shape. It took a while, as if the wood had needed time to get used to his hands. But eventually the saplings stayed where he put them, secure until he could bind them with twine he'd bought from the store.

By noon, Jonah was soaked to the bone, and the wigwam was still hours from being finished. His hands were rubbed raw from handling the wet bark. All the stooping and stretching was making his back hurt. Maybe he should take a break, just for a few minutes, go back into the cabin. It would be dry inside, warm.

No. He had to hold out. What was the matter with

being wet? Nothing! The rain wasn't cold. The air was still warm. The only thing wrong with being wet was the soaked clothes – the jeans, the shirt – acting like a heavy second skin, dragging him down.

He stopped work, dropped the knife, let go of the twine and the green sticks. He looked up, opening his mouth, tasting the rain. His face to the heavens, he took off his shirt, peeling it away from his body. He pulled off the T-shirt underneath, feeling the cool drops on his bare skin. It wasn't enough. He loosened his leather belt, unbuttoned his jeans and shook them to the ground.

Barefoot and nearly naked, he walked down to the lake. The rain got heavier, riddling the sandy beach's damp skin with tiny pock-marks. The lake was a white-capped sheet of gray, but to Jonah it looked as inviting as a tropical pool.

He waded in. The smooth stones and soft sand felt like velvet under the soles of his feet. As he walked deeper and deeper into the lake, the cool water covered his calves, his thighs, and strands of seaweed tickled his body. When the water came up to his chest, he stood still and listened to the raindrops on the water. Gradually, the waves calmed. The clouds broke up, forming new clusters and shapes, showing blade-thin strands of sunlight. Then, coming from behind the tall line of trees that straddled the shoreline beyond the beach, a huge bird – like a giant hawk – swooped toward the water.

Jonah watched, open-mouthed, as the bird flapped its mighty wings – once, twice – and soared in a wide arc over his head. His heart pounding, Jonah reached his arms to the sky, as if he could touch the creature, as if he could run his fingers through its soft underfeathers.

The bird made one last loop – its magnificent head white and brilliant against the dull gray sky – and flew back to land.

Tears stung Jonah's eyes as he watched it disappear.

An eagle, he thought – the greatest symbol of the spirit world. Had it been looking for him? Had it been sent to him – a sign?

He scanned the treetops for another glimpse, but the eagle was gone. Never mind, he thought. There'd be another one. He stretched his arms again, lifted his feet from the sandy bottom and dived across the surface of the lake. The cold water numbed his body, but as he swam towards shore he felt protected, as if the lake itself were a warm cocoon.

He stepped out of the water and onto the sand.

He trudged up the hill and back into the forest. He stood in the clearing, admiring the ash wigwam. Something came to him – he could feel it in the air, hear it in the swaying trees, see it in the clouds. And as he looked up to see if the eagle was perched on a branch above him, Jonah knew. . .

He'd be safe here. In this forest. On this lake.

Chapter Four
—
ETTA

On some stupid talk show, fat couples with perms and mullets were finding out if the mullet guy was the real father of the perm lady's ugly baby. I was sure I'd seen this episode before. At the end of each nail-biting segment, just before the commercials for glycerine suppositories or acid reflux medicine, the host would drawl, 'Randy, you *are* the father,' or 'Darnell, you are *not* the father,' which would usually get lard-assed Darnell out of his seat to do a little victory whoop and dance.

It was during Darnell's celebration that Kyle knocked on the door. That was the first weird thing – he knocked. Usually when he came by he just barged right in. So why the politeness this time? Why did he wait for me to answer the door and let him in before he asked, 'Your ma at home?' And why did he ask, when he knew damn well she wouldn't be at home,

42

that it was a Tuesday, one o'clock in the afternoon, and her shift wasn't over for another two hours. Why? Because he thought I was stupid.

And, I suppose I was, not to have slammed the door in his face and told him to get lost. No, I just let him in.

'So where is she?' He smelled of cigarettes, covered up by Doublemint gum.

'Work.'

'Oh.' He poked his head around the open door, double-checking that the trailer was empty, that there really was nobody at home except me.

'You mind if I wait, then?'

Here comes my second mistake. 'No,' I said. 'Come on in.'

He sat on the couch, next to where I'd been sitting. I plopped down on a chair, as far away from him as possible. I wanted to get out of there and go tell Mom that something was up with her boyfriend, and I could just about guess what it was. Instead, I fiddled with a hole in the upholstery, trying to organise the frayed threads at the edge of the hole into a nice, neat pattern.

'What the hell is this?' On the TV another supersized couple was fighting about who was responsible for their chunky child's fat genes. 'Jesus,' Kyle snorted. 'Imagine going on a show like that. Hanging out all your dirty laundry.'

I didn't tell Kyle, but I *could* imagine going on a show like that, if the title was something like, 'My mom brings home a series of creepy, inappropriate or downright dangerous boyfriends.' I saw programmes like that all the time, but usually the titles were written in shorthand – 'My mom's a slut.'

A commercial came on for a product I'd never heard of before, a pill that was for women who don't like sex. You could go to your doctor and get a prescription. Three women were talking about it – two blonde women who looked happy, a brunette one who didn't. The two blondes figured a couple doses of that stuff and the brunette would be rocking and rolling in no time. I played with the frayed threads, tried not to listen.

'Guess that's why blondes have more fun, huh?' Kyle said.

For the first time in my life, I was glad my hair wasn't any color at all, not even mousy brown, more a dull, khaki beige. I was also glad that Mom had left the air conditioning on all night so I had on my gray sweatpants and a long-sleeved T-shirt.

44

'So what time you say your mom gets back?'

'Any minute now,' I lied, staring at the armchair hole. Straightening out the frayed threads wasn't getting me anywhere, so I started pulling out tiny bits of the cottony upholstery that were showing through.

'Got any smokes?' He got up and started walking around, agitated, opening drawers, digging under the couch cushions.

'Nope.'

'Don't smoke, eh?'

'Nope.

'A good girl, huh?'

'Yeah, I guess.'

'You guess? You mean you don't know?'

I pulled more white fluff out of the chair. If I concentrated on that hard enough, maybe Kyle would just disappear. I heard him fidget on the couch, making the sagging springs squeak underneath him. He got up again, like he was too wired to sit still, like he was impatient, waiting for something.

Then his phone went. The ringtone was some lame oldie – 'Takin' Care of Business'. Kyle looked at the flashing number, pressed a button and put the phone to his ear, listening.

After a few seconds of grunts and mmm-hmms, he looked over at me.

'Fine,' he said, 'Kid's here, though.' Then he was quiet, while the other person talked.

I looked over at the TV again. Another commercial. A white-haired lady was singing the praises of her incontinence pants. Kyle kept watching me, so I stared at the screen, as if nothing was more interesting than adult diapers.

'We're gonna have to wait on that, Charlie. We gotta teach them Chicago guys a lesson. Show people around here we mean business.'

Chicago? What was he talking about? Business? As far as I knew, he didn't even have a job.

'We ain't got a choice, Charlie. That's the only kind of language these people understand.'

Kyle was pacing back and forth in the kitchen, squeaking his shoes on the nice tile floor. He stopped talking, though. A few more 'yeps' and 'nopes' and the call was over. He came back into the living room. I smiled at him, a big stupid grin, like the ones Mom used around men when she needed to play dumb. I wondered if Kyle could tell from the doorway how hard my heart was pounding, how dry my mouth was.

'Want a beer, Etta?' He walked over to the chair. God, he was tall. Way over six feet.

'No, thanks.' *Thanks?* What was the matter with me?

Then he bent over me, got real close, like he was talking to a deaf person or a little kid. I thought he was going to say something about the phone call, about how it wasn't how it sounded, how he wasn't another low-rent criminal like those other guys Mom went out with. That wasn't what was on his mind, though.

'I won't tell your ma,' he whispered. The Doublemint had lost its war with the cigarettes.

I looked down again, my smile all gone. I could see the wood frame of the chair under the big hole I'd dug in the fluff.

'We can do anything we want, you and me. Smoke. Drink. Whatever, you know? I ain't gonna tell.'

What I wanted to do was get the hell out of there – away from Kyle, away from whatever it was he was thinking of doing. But where would I go? Who did I know?

Kyle's breath was hot on my face. Was he going to kiss me? Spit on me? Finally, I came to.

That's it, I thought. I've had enough.

Why was I just sitting here, taking this crap?

'Leave me alone, Kyle.' I tried to get up and push past him, but he grabbed me by the shoulders and shoved me back down in the chair.

'Leave *you* alone,' he said. 'That's a good one.' He was kneeling, face right up close to mine. The smell of his breath was making me feel sick. 'You're the one who ain't leaving *me* alone. You been coming on to *me*, anybody could see that.'

I tried not to look into his eyes. The corner of his mouth had a tiny cut in it. There was pus around the edge of the scab.

'Your ma warned me about you, girl. She said you'd have a go with anybody, even her own mother's boyfriend.'

'*What?*'

'Said you didn't care where you got it from, long as you got the attention.'

'That's crazy,' I hissed.

He had me by the arms now, and was pressing his fingers into my skin, hard enough to leave a mark.

'She told me everything about you, how she had to move you up here to get you away from all the stuff you were getting up to over in Minnesota.'

'That's not true. I wasn't getting up to—'

'You calling her a liar? Your own hard-working mother?'

Finally, I stopped struggling. It was no use. Like a baby, like a weakling, I was about to cry. Then Kyle loosened his grip. He stroked my arms with the palms of his hands, giving them a nice gentle rub, like he was trying to smooth away the pain. Instantly, my nose dried up. The tears didn't fall either. Funny, that.

'Sorry if I got rough,' he said. 'Didn't mean to hurt you. It's just what you said, you know, it kinda pissed me off.'

He walked away from the chair, away from the living room. Strolling into the kitchen, he casually opened the fridge door and took out a beer.

'Don't say nothing to your mom, and I won't say nothing either.' He opened the screen door. 'That's the deal. You got that? Nothing.'

The door closed behind him and he stepped onto the porch.

'Hey, that's quite a collection you got there.' He was talking to somebody outside, his voice light and friendly, a good guy voice. It must have been the weird lady who lived next door and kept a whole display of plastic lawn animals in her tiny yard. She treated them like babies, washing them every day,

49

re-painting the bits that were chipped or faded, taping together any parts that had broken off. She acted like a real mother. How fair was that? Plastic bears and deer had a better parenting deal than me.

'I've had most of these critters a long time.' The neighbor lady was stuttering, surprised by this sudden attention from a charming young man. 'They're part of the family, I guess.'

Curled up in the chair, my throbbing arms wrapped tightly around my body, I listened as the door of Kyle's fancy car opened and closed, as his engine purred and his tires crunched on the gravel driveway.

'Been great talking to you, ma'am,' Kyle shouted to the lady.

Like he was a nice, normal man. Like this was a nice, normal day.

PETER

The passport control area was teeming with armed police and huge Alsatians straining at leather leads. Peter's heart raced. There'd obviously been some sort of security scare – had it involved him? Maybe someone at home had raised the alarm on his credit card fraud. Maybe the bank had spotted something dodgy in the way he'd typed in his dad's password on the computer. Were they able to do that? He knew his father would find out soon enough that he was gone, and how he'd paid for the ticket. But that wouldn't be for days, would it?

The line moved slowly. When it was Peter's turn he shuffled up to a burly woman in a tight-fitting blue uniform, who forced out a smile. He expected a barrage of questioning and had spent much of the flight time rehearsing his answers. He was visiting his uncle, he'd tell them. That wasn't exactly a lie. He was traveling alone because his mother had just died and his father, well, his father wasn't really up to much. Yes, it was cancer. Yes, she was tragically young. His throat had tightened when he'd thought up that line, and he'd imagined a kindly immigration officer wiping away a tear. No, of course he hadn't used his dad's credit card in a fraudulent manner to obtain any financial goods or services. What did they take him for, a thief? Why, he was just a poor, nearly-orphaned fifteen-year-old.

The burly woman stamped his passport and ordered him to have a nice day. There would be no interrogation, no cavity search, no phone calls to Interpol, no deportation. Not yet, anyway.

Peter picked up his holdall and passed through the doors to the main terminal. He scanned the anxious, waiting crowd, but where was his uncle? It didn't help that every man seemed to be dressed in a sort of uniform – baseball caps and white sneakers, brightly-colored T-shirts or polo shirts, new-looking blue jeans or khaki shorts.

'Hey, Pete.'

Uncle Ken lumbered over like a big bear and hugged Peter until he couldn't breathe.

'Great to see you, kid.'

Ken finally let go, thumping Peter's back as if he wanted to expel any tiny air pockets that might still be left in his lungs. Then he took the holdall and guided Peter through the tangle of luggage trolleys, pushchairs, stressed-out passengers, crying children.

When they got to the main concourse, Peter noticed a small old-fashioned aeroplane suspended from the ceiling. On the side of the fuselage was written 'Spirit of St Louis'. Peter had seen this before when he was little, with Mum. He recognized the dull metal body, covered in tiny dents, as if it had been buffeted by rocks and debris.

'That's a replica of Charles Lindbergh's plane.' Ken stopped so Peter could take a long look. 'Kids your age pro'ly don't know who he was, but he was the first guy to fly solo across the Atlantic.'

'Amazing,' Peter said, blankly. He was trying his best to listen, but the terminal building was still packed with security officers and policemen. There were at least a dozen of them, strolling up and down in twos and threes. Was this normal?

'He's still famous around here because he was from Minnesota. Charles Lindbergh. The Lone Eagle, they called him. A real American hero.'

Ken moved on, thankfully, whisking Peter through the airport, past the souvenir shops, the fast food joints, the dark, crowded bars. They rushed by the door to a gents' toilet. Peter was bursting for a pee, but there was no way he was going to stop now. Finally, they reached the end of the long concourse. A set of escalators led down to the car park. Beyond that, there was outside – safety, freedom.

Ken stepped off the escalator and stopped again. Peter nearly tumbled into him. Now what?

'You fixed OK for dollars, Pete?' Ken nodded at a cash machine in the corner.

Dollars? Peter felt sick again.

'We can stop somewhere else, if you want. I just figured, since we're here.'

Money. Jesus. Quick. Lie.

'I'm fine, thanks,' he squeaked, tapping the wallet in the back pocket of his jeans. Inside were two crumpled twenty dollar bills and a handful of quarters.

The automatic doors opened and Peter breathed in the warm exhaust fumes from hundreds of cars.

'Welcome home,' Ken said.

Forty dollars and a bit of change. That would be more than enough, wouldn't it?

JONAH

It rained for the rest of the day, but Jonah's seals held – the wigwam stayed dry. He sat on the floor, naked except for the heavy, woollen blanket he'd taken from home. It was rough and itchy against his skin. A soft leather cloth would have been better, but there weren't too many newly-tanned hides in his mother's bedroom closet.

There he was, thinking about her again, wondering if he should go into the cabin and call her. He wanted to tell her about the things he'd done – building a real wigwam, keeping himself dry and secure with nothing more than the fruits of the forest and the strength and skill of his hands.

She'd probably shrug. 'Why didn't you just go to Target and buy a tent?'

And if he told her about seeing the eagle, she'd just roll her eyes.

There was never anything he could do to break her

down. He tried talking to her about their heritage, but she'd flick his words away with a wave of her hands, make one of the smart-ass remarks that were her specialty.

'You want *heritage*? Go downtown. Hang out with the winos. Plenty of heritage down there.'

Sometimes at dinner, or while they were standing at the sink, washing and drying the dishes, he'd try to wring out stories about her parents or her grandparents. It seemed like a natural time – around the cooking fire, but without the fire.

'Leave it alone, Jonah. If you want some nice, *Dances with Wolves* crap about how great our people lived, you won't get it from me.'

'I don't want that, Mom. I just want the truth.'

'They didn't live great, OK? That's the truth.'

Usually, she'd go quiet on the subject, something she never did otherwise. He should've told her friends or the people she worked with – you ever want my mom to shut up, just ask her about being an Indian. Even better, ask her about her dad.

But one time she got so angry Jonah thought she would hit him. It was this summer, after a pork chop supper and a couple of glasses of red wine. She was at the sink, running the faucet, rinsing the plates, humming to herself. He asked her a question, tried to slip it in, take advantage of her good mood. He couldn't remember what the question was exactly – something about life on the reservation.

'Why don't you give me a break, Jonah?'

She spoke very slowly, but he could hear something simmering in the back of her throat.

'Seriously, Jonah.' She picked up a plate, turned around to face him and let the plate slip through her fingers and shatter onto the floor. 'Why don't you just give me a *fucking* break.' Another plate went onto the floor. Then the salad bowl.

'I'm sorry, Mom, it's OK, just stop that now.'

She threw things across the room – glasses, bowls, knives, forks – over and over, opening drawers, emptying cupboards, and all the time she was screaming at him.

'You are *not* an Indian, Jonah, you hear me? Your father was white. White, Jonah. White. You're not even *half* an Indian because one of my grandfathers was white.'

She kept on until she'd smashed everything. Then she stomped over to the back door and opened it, sweeping her arms like she wanted him to leave.

'You go. Go to any tribe, go to any reservation. Tell

them about your *heritage* or your *blood* and see what they do. They'd just laugh at you, a stupid half-white boy who doesn't know how lucky he is, how lucky he is not to be a fucking. . .'

She shook her head. It was like she couldn't even say the word.

And then she cried. She sat at the kitchen table and cried until it looked like her face would crumble, collapse into itself like a flood-damaged building. Jonah stood in the doorway, too angry and hurt to comfort her, too shocked at the hateful, shameful power of her words.

After a while she tried to talk. Something about boarding schools and Vietnam and someone being a drunk and dying at fifty, but the words weren't coming out right and Jonah had been in no mood to hear them.

Two months later and what she'd done still felt like an open wound.

Jonah wrapped the blanket around his waist and stepped outside the wigwam. The rain had stopped, although soft drops still filtered through the branches and leaves of the trees. The air was like perfume, sweet and herby, warm and moist. He took deep breaths, as if the fragrance could heal his memories, take away their sting. And if it couldn't, what did it matter? He lived here now. The earth was his mother. Yellow Lake was his home.

Chapter Five
—
ETTA

Friday night. Three whole days since Kyle caught me alone in the trailer, and he hadn't been around since. Maybe Mom got wise to him. Maybe she told him where he could stick it.

We were having dinner, takeout pizza in front of the TV, watching *Friends*, and Mom was laughing out loud at the way Monica was bouncing off the furniture in a fat suit. Normally, Kyle would come around on a Friday. It was weird that she didn't mention him, so when a commercial came on I asked her if something was up.

'Up?' Mom asked. She sounded normal, relaxed. She bit into her piece of pizza, wiped some sauce from her chin. 'What do you mean, up?'

'I mean, did you guys break up or something?'

'No, he's just busy is all. He's starting some deal with these guys from Kenosha.'

I didn't say any more. I let the big sale announcement for Menard's Lumber Warehouse take up the silence. If Mom didn't want to talk about it, then that was OK.

Only she *did* want to talk.

'You know, like a *business*.' Mom's voice sounded a little higher than normal. 'A factory. Making stuff. OK?'

I wanted to ask her what kind of stuff, but I knew how she'd take it. Turned out, my *not* asking made her take it the same way. After a few seconds she picked up the remote and turned down the sound.

'It's all on the up-and-up, Etta. A business opportunity. Car parts or something.'

I kept my mouth shut. Car parts, right.

'Can't you give the guy a break?' she screeched.

'What are you talking about, Mom? I didn't say anything!'

She threw down her pizza and folded her arms. 'You didn't need to. I can tell what you're thinking.'

'That's crazy, Mom.'

'No, it ain't.'

'Yes it is.'

She was acting like a five-year-old, so she must have known something was wrong – with that business, with me. When the show came back on she turned the sound up so loud the laugh track hurt my ears. I should have taken the remote off her and made her listen, for a change. I should've told her about Kyle calling me a slut. I should have tried squeezing *her* arm till it bruised, seen how she liked it. I should've told her what I heard him say on the phone to some guy named Charlie, that stupid gangster stuff about 'lessons'.

But she wouldn't even look at me, let alone talk. She stared at the TV like her eyes had got stuck in that position and wouldn't ever move.

'OK,' I said, sarcastically. 'Sorry I even asked.' I made a big show of stomping out of the trailer and letting the door slam behind me. It felt good, hearing the metal steps shudder and shake, made me feel like I was a normal everyday teenager, one with normal, everyday problems and a normal, everyday mom.

I ran down the bike trail, headed into Welmer. It was like being the last survivor in one of those movies about the end of the world. The houses were all dark, the streets empty. When I got to town I walked right in the middle of the road, just like in the movies. There was nobody to stop me. No one to even see.

Then a car came up the road, swerving back and

forth, catching me in its headlights, forcing me to skip onto the sidewalk. It drove past, slowed down so the boys inside could lean over for a quick gawk before speeding up and skidding around the next left turn.

I turned right on Main Street, walked past a boarded-up store and a tavern with no lights on. I took another right at the next corner – not that I cared what direction I was going in. I had nowhere to go. The houses on this street were small, with tiny toy-covered front lawns and open square porches. There were warm yellow lights on in some of them. I saw the wallpaper in a kid's room. Disney Princesses, pink and pretty. I don't know why that made me jealous. I hated Disney. I hated pink even more.

I slowed down, dragging my feet along the sidewalk, dipping the toes of my sneakers into the cracks in the pavement. I had to make a plan. I couldn't just walk around in circles all night. I needed to think things through. What if I told Mom everything and she took Kyle's side? What if she thought I was making it up? What if she *had* been telling everybody I was some kind of slut? Those questions kept going round and round in my head. Worse ones, too. What if she was in on something with him, something really bad this time – something dangerous or illegal, not just stupid?

The car full of boys turned back onto the street. They crossed the center line, slowed down, pulled over onto the grass, nearly cutting off the sidewalk, blocking my way. It was nice car – new, metallic blue, just like Kyle's.

'Hey.' The driver's head bobbed out of the open window. Country music was blasting out of the speakers. Some deep-voiced hick was whining about trains. 'You're that chick from the trailer court.' The boy was wearing a baseball cap that said, 'Welmer Panthers. All-State Basketball Champs.' He didn't look too bad, a little shiny and pimply was all.

The guy in the passenger seat leaned over for a better look. He had a long, skinny face, and bleached blonde hair under a Minnesota Twins cap. His tiny eyes were glazed over, either drunk or high.

'We seen you down by the football field that time,' he mumbled. Both boys were messed up, but at least they were smiling. Maybe I should do what Mom said, give them a break.

'We got beer,' the driver said. The two boys in the back seat raised their Leinenkugel cans in a kind of salute. 'Other shit too.'

'And we got a place to do it.' The driver revved the car engine for effect.

'You wanna go there?' More revving, louder this time. 'It ain't far.'

'No, thanks.'

'Christ Almighty,' the front seat guy said. 'Ain't you stuck-up?'

'I gotta go home,' I said.

'Think you're too good for us or something?' the driver asked.

'Honest, guys, I just gotta go.' I sounded like Mom, kissing some loser's butt.

'What you getting so high and mighty about, anyway? You're the one living in the trailer park.'

The guys in the back seat laughed, choking on their beer until it spewed out of their mouths like foamy fountains. One of them chucked his empty can out of the window. It clattered on the sidewalk next to my feet.

'Thanks for reminding me,' I said, picking up the can and backing away from the car. 'I might've gone to the wrong house if you hadn't pointed that out.'

From inside the car, one of the boys shouted, 'Smart-ass, ain't ya?'

I scrunched up the can with my fingers. There

was no point in wasting any more of my words.

'Bitch!' The car pulled away clumsily, no squealing tires, no gravel dust. It was a let-down, really, but still they kept shouting. 'Bitch. Whore.' They called me the other name, too – the *really* nasty one.

I wound my arm back and let the can fly. It took off like a cannon ball, soaring through the air, catching the light, until it clunked straight onto the blacktop, short by a mile.

Ten minutes later and I was back at home. Mom had left the living room light on for me. She'd cleared away the pizza and put the box in the garbage. My uneaten pieces were on a plate on the counter, neatly wrapped in aluminum foil. There was a post-it note on the top.

Day off tomorrow. How about Duluth?

That made me smile. Maybe she wasn't so bad.

I finished off my pizza and went to bed. For a long time I lay awake in the dark, thoughts niggling in my head. It was about those stupid boys in the car, something they had said.

Just after midnight, it came to me. It wasn't what they had said or the names they had called me.

It was the car – same make as Kyle's, same color as Kyle's.

I could see it now, pulling away. I'd been too angry and upset to notice it before. There were bumper stickers on the back, side by side – one Harley Davidson logo, one American flag.

Same as Kyle's.

PETER

The alarm clock read 2:00 a.m. It wouldn't be light for another two hours. Peter lay on Ken's living room sofa, eyes closed, trying not to think about things so he could get back to sleep.

Uncle Ken's flat – Ken called it a 'condo' – was in a brand new building, with white walls, bare wooden floors and what Mum used to call that 'new motel' smell. Peter had never been in a new motel, but he knew what she meant – unused, sanitary, too clean for Mum's taste – and smelling it made him think of her. He looked up at the ceiling, wondering if she was thinking of him too. He knew it was mad, but he couldn't help it. He felt her eyes on him sometimes, and he imagined her, dressed as normal in jeans and T-shirt, peering down on him through a telescope from a very high cloud.

Peter thought about his dad, too. He'd still be in Italy, basking beside some pool. What time would

68

it be there? He checked his watch. 10:00 in England, an hour later in Italy. Dad would be home in a few more days. At least nobody had called yet – no police, nobody in England, wondering where he'd gone. His aunt Emma was supposed to be checking in on him. She must've believed his text that said he was staying at his mate Luke's for a few days. Luke and his family were on holiday and wouldn't answer their phone, so that might hold her till Dad got back.

Outside a car alarm went off and a dog started to bark. Peter pulled the pillow over his head to drown out the sound.

It was no use. He tossed and turned for a few minutes, then finally gave up. He pulled on his jeans and shirt and crept through the darkened flat to the balcony. Ken's condo overlooked the Mississippi River. It was too dark to see, and too noisy with the hum of air conditioners to hear, but from the balcony Peter could at least *smell* the Mississippi, earthy and brown.

He wondered if the river would lead to Yellow Lake. He supposed it would, eventually. That's how rivers worked, right? Maybe he should take off now – he'd already wasted enough time in Minneapolis – go down to the riverside, see if there was anyone with a boat for hire. It was worth a try. Or he could hitchhike. Yellow Lake wasn't all that far from Minneapolis. He had money for a map, he could take some food, buy a little more – he'd be at the cabin in a matter of hours. He could leave a note for Ken, explain that he couldn't sleep, that he'd decided to beat the rush hour, something daft like that.

He took in a deep breath of the sweet moldy river. He looked up at the night sky, at the stars twinkling, a half moon hiding behind a bank of clouds. He closed his eyes and saw Mum again, looking down, only this time she was looking away from her telescope and rolling her eyes at his pathetic idea.

She was right. Leaving now would only lead to worry, to questions, to phone calls home. He'd have to be patient, as hard as that was. He'd have to stay cooped up in the condo until Ken dropped him off at the bus station on his way to work.

He went back into the living room and sat on the sofa. He picked up the holdall from the floor and rummaged through his pants and socks, digging until he found the satin bag that held the bit of Mum's hair.

When he looked at the thin piece of cloth, he felt even more of an idiot. Mum was probably up on that cloud, laughing her head off with one of her angel mates.

'Doesn't he realize that it was a joke?' she'd guffaw. 'What does he think *that*'s going to achieve?'

Peter put the bag back in its hiding place. He zipped up the holdall, gave it a pat.

No, he thought. Mum hadn't been joking. She wouldn't laugh.

He lay down on the sofa and pulled the covers over his head. As long as the phone didn't ring, he'd be OK. As long as the doorbell didn't go, as long as there were no police cars pulling up outside the condo, they'd get to Yellow Lake.

Just the two of them, as he'd promised.

JONAH

The moon was full and from the opening of the wigwam Jonah could just make out the cabin. It no longer tormented him with the promise of comfort and warmth, of beds and blankets. Since he'd finished the wigwam, he had no need for it.

He closed his eyes. The night sounds were like music. The lapping of the lake water against the shore, the hum of insects, the whooshing sway of trees, the sharp cry of a bird, the crunch and shuffle of nocturnal creatures. This was what heaven sounded like. There weren't any trumpets, or brassy choirs or clanging cymbals. Heaven sounded like nature, heaven sounded like earth.

Yawning, bone-tired after another day's hard work, Jonah lowered the sheet that was his front door and lay down on the mat that he'd managed to weave for himself. He covered his aching body with the blanket he'd brought from home and drifted blissfully into sleep.

Then – how long had he been sleeping? – he was awake again. What woke him up? A light filtered into the wigwam, but it wasn't the sunrise. Not yet.

Headlights.

On. Then off, so there was darkness again. On again.

A car door slammed. Voices were raised – louder, until they became shouts. It was men – angry or drunk. Maybe both.

Somebody's found me, Jonah thought.

It would be like being at school again – a hard wall, tile over concrete, his skull seeming soft and pliable, easily re-shaped into another form.

'Hey!'

Slow down, he willed his thoughts. Nobody knows you're here. Slow down. Be quiet.

'Hey, you son of a bitch.'

Hush. He forced his lungs to stop pushing out the air so loudly, commanded his heart to stop its dangerous hammering. Listen.

'I'm talking to you, asshole.'

A laugh. A deeper voice. 'Who you calling asshole, asshole?'

Whoever it was out there, they weren't talking to him. Jonah heard a loud belch, then someone gagging and retching.

'Hey, dude. Kyle ain't gonna like it that you puked on his car.'

Who were these people? They must all be drunk or high on something. They sounded young too, as if their voices hadn't completely changed. The sound they made together was like a gaggle of low-flying geese.

Suddenly, the voices stopped. Although he couldn't *hear* the men, he could feel their presence like a huge shadow inching towards the wigwam, a silently spreading black stain. This was it, he told himself. This was the end. There was no way he could fight off four of them, even if they were stoned out of their minds. He inched his body towards the back of the wigwam, shielded himself with his blanket and mat.

Wait! This was stupid. Fear was making him weak. He dug into the ground and found a cord that was keeping the sides of the wigwam pegged to the ground. He could take out two of the supporting stakes and lift up a section of soft bark. He could slide underneath on his stomach, crawl into the woods and hide out till morning. They'd be gone by then.

Outside an empty beer can rattled on a solid surface. They were near the cabin, on the narrow pavement near the door or on the side patio.

Jonah heard drunken whispers, stifled laughter. The sounds of shuffling and shoving, of muffled instructions, grew louder until he could make out garbled words.

'Harder.'

'Come on.'

'Do it again.'

They were breaking in. They weren't on the lookout for an Indian kid they'd seen in town buying twine and canvas at Hardware Hank. They weren't racist goons, or right wing militia members, ready to teach a trespassing Indian a lesson, white-boy style. They were just stupid local kids using the cabin as a place to party.

Jonah heard a crash, as the cabin's door was finally broken down. He crept away from the corner, pulled back the door sheet and peered out. Maybe he should try to stop them. No. He'd be outnumbered. What about the phone? He could sneak inside, call the police, report a break-in. But what if the cops searched the whole area? What if they found the wigwam, found *him*?

Jonah laid the mat flat again, stretched out, pulled the blanket over his head. The cabin wasn't his responsibility. Some white man built a house that he wasn't even prepared to live in, while all over the world, the poor and homeless festered in slums and shanty towns.

If trespassers wrecked the place, then the owner got what he deserved.

From outside, another light darted across the back of the wigwam. Another car door opened and closed. Jonah was nearly asleep again, not sure if what he was hearing was real or part of a jumbled-up dream. Something else had arrived, someone bigger, older, stronger, with footsteps that shook the ground.

It sounded like the Windigo, Jonah thought, the starving giant who preyed on the young, and devoured their flesh to satisfy his eternal hunger. He struggled to stay awake, in case the Windigo attacked.

No, stupid. The Windigo wasn't real. He was just an Ojibwe legend, a symbol for evil, a story his mother told him once to scare him, to make him behave. There was no such thing as the Windigo, no such thing as. . .

He yawned.

The sounds outside the wigwam faded away. Real or fantasy, awake or dreaming – it didn't matter any more. It was too late. He was too tired. Jonah curled over onto his side and fell back to sleep.

Chapter Six
ETTA

Mom and I were on the road by 9:30. It was as if last night had never happened.

The fall was still a long way off, but the tops of the trees we were driving past were changing color, like they'd been dusted with red and gold frosting. Maybe it was just the sun's reflection, but it seemed like a sign – this was going to be one of those days when everything would go right. The car wouldn't break down on the way to the mall. We'd find what we wanted in the stores, in just the right size, and all on sale – fifty per cent off. The cashier would accept Mom's credit card, smile and say, 'Thank you for shopping with us, ladies.'

I was almost woozy with excitement. It reminded me of when I was little, when there was no boyfriend around to take her away from me. We'd be like sisters, laughing and giggling, and she'd be acting silly, just for fun, not to get the attention of some man.

She glanced over at me, and smiled. 'We should get you some lipstick today. You've got such pretty lips.' She took her right hand off the steering wheel for a second just to touch my mouth. 'You got them from your dad, you know? He didn't have much going for him, but he had really pretty lips. Nice eyes, too.'

I looked in the mirror. I *did* have pretty lips. My cheekbones seemed to be getting higher, too, and it looked like my nose was getting shorter. Was that possible? Did these kinds of things happen right before you turned fifteen?

Like I said, things just seemed perfect. I loved it when she talked about my dad. He was no better than any of the other 'regulars', I knew that. He was probably no better even than Kyle, but, well, he was my father and that was important to me. I tried to think of some way to keep on the subject – she never told me anything about him, except that his name was Jack and he spent some time in jail right after I was born, and that he was always stealing our stuff to sell so he could buy cocaine. That was why there weren't any baby pictures of me anywhere, except the studio ones that Grandpa must have paid for. Whenever Mom got hold of a camera, my dad would steal it or some dealer would break in and just snatch it away. That was also why my only memories of watching TV were from when I was at Grandpa and the Duchess's house. Anything we had, we didn't have for long.

Mom and I were listening to an oldies station on the radio. The reception wasn't good because there were power lines next to the road, and the trees were too tall. We could only get three stations clear enough to really hear. One was country, one was some lunatic talk show, so we had to go with the oldies. Most of the songs that crackled through the speakers were from way before I was born – Prince, Janis Joplin, the Rolling Stones – but Mom knew the words to every one of them. When we got close to Duluth a Bob Dylan song came on. I couldn't make out the lyrics because Mom was shrieking along, but I got the idea. It was all about having everything when you were young, and then being so poor and lonely when you grew up that you couldn't even figure out how to get back home.

'Story of my life,' she said when the song was over. We rounded a sharp bend and the road dipped down into a narrow hollow. We lost the reception, so she turned the radio off. 'I mean, that's how my life used to be, when I was your age and I lived at home with

Grandpa and the Duchess. I had anything I wanted – expensive clothes, a nice car. . .'

I waited for her to say more, about her life, about growing up a rich cheerleader type and ending up in a trailer. I looked out at the copper-topped trees flying past, felt my stomach do a little flip when the road leapt suddenly up out of the hollow and onto the flat land again.

Nothing. The conversation just stopped. I shouldn't have been surprised, though. She hardly ever told me stories unless, like today, a song would come on that reminded her of something, and she'd let a little detail slip out by accident, like it was a dirty secret she was sworn not to tell.

So we kept quiet the rest of the way. It should have been the perfect time to tell her that stuff about Kyle. I could've told her that a bunch of stoned kids were out driving his car last night. Maybe she'd know who they were. Maybe she'd have some explanation.

But that old Dylan song brought us down to earth with a nasty bump, and pushed us back into our own separate worlds. And I knew what had happened the night before, when I just mentioned Kyle's name.

I didn't want anything to ruin our day, especially not him.

And nothing did spoil it. Everything was perfect.
I even got that lipstick. Revlon, Frosted Pink Cherry
in a glossy golden tube, $7.95.

It was later, that night, when everything turned
from shiny to black.

PETER

Peter stared out of the passenger window at the jammed traffic on the motorway. Miles of oversized cars were plodding down the highway like dinosaurs. Uncle Ken looked straight ahead at the line in front of his SUV.

'I shoulda gone to the funeral,' he said. There was something tight in his voice, as if he were going to cry. 'I regret that now. And I ain't just saying that because you're here.'

On the opposite carriageway, Peter watched as a black diplodocus nearly collided with a shiny blue stegosaurus.

'She was my only sister.'

Uncle Ken wiped his nose with the palm of his hand sideways, to make it seem like the casual brushing away of some dust or a bug. 'I shoulda gone.'

Peter's bus to Yellow Lake would be leaving in a few minutes. Ken had bought the ticket online –

his treat, he said, because he felt so bad about not driving Peter there himself. The trip would take all day. He'd need to ride to Duluth, then cut back to Hayward, and over to some other little towns that had 'Lake' in the name. Once he got to Welmer, he'd be able to get a lift out to the cabin. Duane at the grocery store owed Ken a favor. All Peter had to do was ask.

Ken turned off the cross-town freeway and drove down a quieter local road, lined with small wooden houses fronted with neatly-mown lawns and small flower beds.

'Sure you can't wait till next week? I got a couple days of leave owing. I could drive you up. Wouldn't be any big deal.'

Peter looked at Ken and sighed.

'By then I'll be back in England.' He was getting good at this, making up rubbish on the spur of the moment. 'Start of the school term. New beginnings. All that.'

They got to the bus station, just as the Duluth bus pulled in.

Uncle Ken took a map out of the glove compartment and showed him the route, tracing the bus ride with his finger. Highway sixty-one, then down onto thirty-five, then county roads named with letters, not numbers.

'A couple years ago they changed our road from D to DD,' Ken said. 'Your mom thought that was real funny. Like the road was getting a boob job or something.'

Ken's voice got tight again. He sniffed a couple times.

'Now you got the keys, right?' Ken wiped his nose, getting straight back to business.

'I've got the keys.'

They got out of the car and Ken hoisted Peter's holdall out of the boot

'And you sure you don't want to take my cell phone? Piss-poor reception up there, but still. . .'

'I'll be fine.'

'I know it's a pretty tame place – you won't have any trouble – but call me from the landline soon as you get to the cabin, OK?'

They joined the huddle of passengers waiting for the bus driver to finish his cigarette. Ken patted Peter's shoulders, and then gave him another lung-clearing hug.

'Your mom loved that cabin. It always was more hers than mine.'

The driver flicked his cigarette butt onto the

tarmac and crushed it with his foot. He closed the door to the luggage hold, sold a ticket to a mother with two young children. Ken and Peter had time for a final hand-shake while the driver opened the door and started the engine.

'Listen. I haven't been to Yellow Lake for a while,' Ken said. 'Couple of years. I don't really have the inclination to go any more. Duane checked up on it for me this summer, but, well, the cabin might be looking kinda run-down is all.'

The driver revved the engine and Peter stepped onto the bus.

'Just to warn you,' Uncle Ken said.

JONAH

When Jonah woke up, it felt as though the wigwam had turned into a sweat lodge. The sun had been out for hours – what time was it? Why had he slept so long?

Last night. It took a few seconds for the memory to kick in – the slamming car doors, the wasted kids. He sat up, pulling his blanket up to his chest. He rummaged around the wigwam floor for his discarded pair of jeans. He pulled them on – if anybody was still out there, at least he wouldn't be confronting them naked.

He crept outside, tiptoed to the edge of the woods.

No cars. That was good.

Maybe he'd imagined it. Had it had all been part of a bad dream – the shouting, the swearing, the breaking glass?

No. In front of the cabin there were empty cans, broken pieces of wood. And there were tire tracks on the lawn. The front door was wide open too. Somebody *had* broken in.

Jonah stepped across the broken glass and the splintered planks. He crept through the smashed-up door and into the kitchen. The smells hit him first. A burning smell, but not fire. Rubber? Chemicals? Maybe some appliance had blown – had the fridge's motor burned out?

He went into the living room.

What had happened? Chairs were turned over and mattresses were spread across the floor. The oak dining table had been used as a giant ashtray – at least, something had been burned on it. Crushed, empty cans and bits of broken glass were strewn over the furniture and on the floor, along with bits of tubing and empty metal containers – what on earth were they?

And that smell – metallic, burning – was even stronger here.

He opened the door to the lakeside porch and sat down on the steps. Everything seemed so peaceful from here. The lake was smooth as glass, not a ripple on the surface. The air was motionless, the trees were still, the animals were quiet.

Inside the cabin, something crashed to the ground. Jonah jumped to his feet. Quick – what could he use as a weapon? There was a basket of damp firewood beside the porch. He picked up the longest piece he could find. He looked inside the living room – nothing had changed, nobody was there. He opened the screen door and moved toward the kitchen. His heart pounding, both hands clutching the wood like a club, he tiptoed around the pieces of glass, stepped over a yellow and frothy stain on the floor, peered through the doorway, ready to strike. . .

Nothing – no invaders, no thieves. An empty glass jar had shattered on the floor, that was all.

What an idiot I must look like, he thought. Brandishing a two-foot piece of rotting elm against gravity or the wind.

He put down his makeshift club and picked some of the glass. Almost by instinct, as if his mother were there telling him what to do and how to do it, he found a mop and a broom, dug heavy-duty green garbage bags out of a kitchen drawer. He put furniture back into place, swept the floor, even mopped up some kid's red-chunked puke. He made everything nice again, made everything clean.

When he was finished, he fixed the lock and nailed a piece of plywood over the broken door. He spent hours on it, but all the time he was hammering and sawing, he couldn't stop thinking that those boys would be back. And his pathetic repairs – what good would they be then? What good were planks and nails against small town kids with nothing better to do than get wasted and destroy things? What good were flimsy barriers against the cancer that these people spread? Drunken stupidity and drug-fuelled vandalism.

God, he hated them.

And he hated himself. Some Ojibwe, the way he'd gone all through the cabin, broom in hand, like a maid. And last night, the way he'd cowered in the wigwam while these yahoos invaded his territory. *His* territory – that's what it was. The cabin should never have been built, but it was still standing on *his* land, next to *his* hard-built wigwam. But, like a scared little kid, he'd stayed inside and let a bunch of high school losers have the run of the place.

Well, it wouldn't happen again – he'd make sure of that. Next time, he'd take them on. The next time a white person set foot on his territory, he'd fight back, one way or another.

At the end of the day, the white world was finally locked up and put aside, hidden away like a box of nasty tricks that could no longer draw him in.

He went deep into the forest and gathered plants – wild honeysuckle, lady's slipper, some nice-smelling weeds that at least *looked* like sacred sweetgrass. After they were dry he'd burn them on the beach, make a thanksgiving offering.

As he laid the herbs carefully on the wigwam floor, he felt hunger pangs – sharp and painful, as if he'd swallowed an invisible knife. He held out as long as he could before he ate dinner – a stick of beef jerky wrapped up in a cold, dry tortilla. His teeth gnawed the leathery meat, bringing unwelcome reminders of other food – warm meatballs and gravy for Sunday dinner, his mother's home-made lasagne. As he sat alone in the darkening wigwam, he thought about the parties they used to have – his mother's friends and their kids, the bottles of wine at the table, the conversations and card games, the telling of stories and laughing until late in the night.

After he finished his food, he took off his jeans and T-shirt, covered himself with his blanket and lay down to sleep. He listened for sounds – not just the hum of insects or the bark of distant dogs, but human noise. In the days since he left Minneapolis, he'd grown used to the quiet. He could pick things out –

bird calls, the lapping of the waves on the beach, the low growl of an outboard motor across the lake.

Now he listened for traffic out on the black-topped county road, and reached for the piece of firewood that he'd used as a weapon. What if the intruders came back? They'd wonder who fixed the smashed lock. Wouldn't they guess that somebody was living close by? Wouldn't they put two and two together and search the woods?

No. They weren't that smart. They were so stupid, they probably wouldn't even be able to find the place again.

Jonah shifted his body to get comfortable on the hard ground. Other thoughts crept into his mind – people again. A girl he'd met at the class party before school finished. What was her name? He couldn't remember. He could only remember her face. How pretty she was, with chestnut hair and big brown eyes. Her sweet voice, and the way she listened so closely to every word he said. He tried not to think about her now, about wanting to talk to her, wanting to kiss her, wanting to touch her hair, wanting. . .

He tried not to think about how lonely he was.

Chapter Seven
—
ETTA

Night.

Mom got called in to work a late waitress shift. We'd already had a long day, but Saturday night was the best for tips so no way could she turn down a chance to work the dining room. It meant $100 minimum, Mom said, cash in hand, way more than she ever got just cleaning the rooms.

I made us some macaroni and cheese – the real kind, not the mix stuff from a box – while Mom took a quick shower, put her hair up in a bun, rubbed out a couple stains on the housekeeping dress that she hadn't washed yet.

While she was wolfing down her food, she tried calling Kyle. She turned away from me while she left her message, like not seeing her face meant I couldn't hear what she said.

'Hey, hon, it's me.'

How could she get her voice to go so high-pitched and girly?

'I just wanted you to know that I won't be in tonight, so I'll see you when I see you, OK?'

When she put her phone into her purse she looked at me and shrugged, as if to say, 'A girl has to do what a girl has to do.' Then she gave me a kiss and bounced out the door, humming to herself, like someone who was happy, like someone who didn't have a care in the world.

The sound brought back the feeling I'd had in the morning, driving to Duluth. Whatever happened between Mom and me, we'd work things out – just the two of us. The men that kept getting in the way – the Kyles – weren't important. They were just a silly phase that she'd grow out of one day.

I fell asleep watching TV and woke up about midnight. I went into the bathroom to get ready for bed. The new lipstick we'd bought at the Duluth Walmart was still in the bag, stashed in the vanity drawer. I don't know why I thought this would be a good time to try it on. Maybe it was because I was alone – there wouldn't be any witnesses.

The lipstick looked odd at first – too bright, unnaturally frosty like bubblegum ice cream that had silver glitter sprinkled on top. It made me laugh, and that gave me another idea. I'd rummage around Mom's make-up and try on some other stuff, just for fun. So on it went, the thick foundation – a shade too dark, just the way Mom wore it – the lilac eyeshadow, the jet-black eyeliner, the thick, gloopy mascara.

It was funny. Mom was always trying to get me to wear this stuff. She was constantly telling me to 'accent my femininity' by wearing skirts and tighter tops to show off my 'assets', but I always resisted. Now, looking in the mirror, I knew why. Make-up didn't make me look feminine, it made me look like a freak. I didn't look like a grown-up woman. I looked like a male cartoon character – Bugs Bunny or Eric Cartman – dressed up in girls' clothes to trick somebody.

I was about to rub it all off with face cream when the kitchen door slammed. I heard footsteps and weird noises – metal clangs that sounded like pots and pans banging, glasses tinkling, drawers being pulled out and utensils clattering onto the floor. I knew straight away that it wasn't Mom, but who'd break into our trailer and steal our cooking stuff?

'Yo!' Kyle's voice. 'Anybody home?'

I locked the door and turned off the faucet.

'Hey.' Too late. Footsteps came down the hall. 'You in there, honey?'

'It's me, Etta. Mom's at work.'

He must have known that. I'd heard her make the call.

I waited for an answer. 'Kyle?'

I heard men's voices in the kitchen and stuff being moved around.

'Kyle? Is that you?'

Nothing. Just breathing, shuffling. What the hell was he doing? It had to be Kyle, but why didn't he answer?

I stepped away from the door. The room started to wobble so I steadied myself with the edge of the bathtub until I could sit down on the toilet. I put my head between my legs and took deep breaths. Good. That was better. I'd just have to stay here till Mom got home. She could deal with this, she'd know what to do.

Then I thought, no, Mom would think it was crazy to be so scared. She'd never hide out in the bathroom just because of some guy. She'd laugh at me for being such a wuss.

I stood up and listened again – just that low

murmuring from the kitchen. I took in another deep breath, tried to relax. Maybe Kyle was already gone, or maybe he was waiting politely for me to come out, like any normal person would do. Maybe he'd have a reasonable explanation for what he was up to, like any normal person. This was only Kyle. It wasn't the big bad wolf, it wasn't a zombie, it wasn't that guy in *The Shining*, ready to kill me with an axe.

Just my mom's boyfriend.

I opened the door.

Kyle was waiting, flashing his teeth. *Here's Johnny.*

PETER

Why hadn't he brought the stupid phone? Even if there'd been no reception, he could've used the light as a makeshift torch. It was too dark to read the map, too dark to see the road. There were no houses in the distance with warm, welcoming lights to guide him. There was no kindly old lady waiting for a young man lost on the moors to come in and sit by the fire, while she prepared a steaming bowl of chicken soup or porridge.

The bus dropped him off in Welmer in the late afternoon. It wasn't a bad place – it had a high street with older-looking brick buildings and pubs with names like The Bait Shop and The Fish Bowl. The names of the beers were funny, too. Peter wished he'd brought his camera to take pictures of the signs – Hamms, Pabst, Schmidt. *Leinenkugel*, now that was a random name. But who would he have shown them to? Dad wouldn't laugh. Even before, in the good old days, Dad wouldn't have laughed – only Mum.

He went to the supermarket and asked for Duane, just like Ken had told him to.

'What?' The chubby girl at the check-out twitched her head slightly, as if he were speaking a foreign language.

'Duane,' Peter said, trying to add a bit of a twang.

'Oh, *Duane*,' the girl said. 'He don't own this place no more.' She twiddled her varnished, inch-long nails on the black plastic conveyer belt. There was a customer behind him and a line building up.

'Is there a taxi rank in the village?' It was worth a try.

'A *what*?'

So, instead of getting a lift, he walked to County DD and stuck out his thumb. After all, the cabin was only a few miles from town, according to Ken. It would be no time at all before some kind, curious soul from Welmer offered him a lift, drove him along the darkening country roads, dropped him off at the top of the cabin's driveway with a wave or a smile.

He hiked for a mile – no one. Another mile, and he got passed by a battered lorry full of kids, who only slowed down long enough to throw an empty lager can at him. By the third mile the sun had set.

With the darkness came exhaustion. It had been a long day. It'd been hours since he'd had anything proper to eat. Now, struggling along the side of the road, his bag of food and clothing getting heavier and heavier, having no idea how much further he had to walk, he wanted nothing more than to just lie down in the ditch and go to sleep.

He looked up at the starry sky.

'Keep going.' Mum's voice in his head. Great, now she was talking to him. 'You never know what's around the next bend.'

ETTA

I should have slammed the door, locked it again, cowered in the tub until Kyle was gone.

'Hey, Etta.' His smile was still blazing when I stepped out of the bathroom, and he was using his nice guy voice. I got a big hug, too, like he was happy to see me.

'Your mom said you went up to Duluth.' He let go a little, stepped back so he could look at me. His hands were still on my shoulders, holding them so I couldn't move.

'We're back now,' I said. I tried to sound casual, as if there was nothing scary going on, as if men invaded our house all the time. 'Mom'll be home any minute.'

'Great,' he said. He let go of one shoulder, tightened up his grip on the other one, using it to herd me down the hall.

In the kitchen, two men were standing behind the counter. One of them was the skinny weasel-faced boy I'd seen in Kyle's car the night before. The other guy was older, with a fat stomach and a red face, and a flabby neck that was covered in pimples.

They had stuff spread out in front of them like they were working in a store. Metal cans – that must have been the clanging. Clear plastic bags filled with powdery stuff. A big pile of crumpled-up money.

My stomach flipped. This was bad.

'Hey, Charlie, look who's here.'

Charlie, the fat guy, looked me up and down and grunted something. The weasel kid grabbed one of the bags of yellowy powder, hid it behind his back.

'You don't have to do that.' Kyle's fingers moved down from my shoulder to my arm. He squeezed the same place where he'd bruised me before. The pain traveled through my skin, into my muscles, all the way down to the bone.

'You ain't seen nothing, have you, Etta?'

I shook my head. Kyle eased up on his grip.

'Good.' He reached down to the floor, picked up a duffle bag, and tossed it to the kid, who started putting away all the counter stuff.

Kyle took my arm again, gentler this time, and led me towards the door, still smiling, still sounding nice.

'We just need you to come with us while we run a little errand for your mom,' he said.

'What kind of errand?'

Kyle opened the door for me, led me down the steps. From behind me, a blubbery hand brushed against my butt.

'She wants us to drop off some stuff at the hotel and give her a lift home.'

Kyle's car was parked right in front, the engine running. There were more men inside. I couldn't tell how many.

'Why can't I wait here?'

Kyle was opening the back door, guiding me in.

'She wants you to come along. That's what she said. You can ask her yourself when we get there.'

I knew he was lying. He *had* to be lying, but I went with them, like he told me to. I didn't scream, I didn't try to run away. I just climbed into the back seat, behind Kyle and the driver, got squashed in between the skinny kid and the pimply fatso.

As the car pulled out of the trailer park, I looked straight ahead. I kept my legs tight together and my arms crossed. Beside me, Charlie's breath was heavy and wheezy, like he'd just come back from a run. The driver fiddled with the radio for a minute, but there was nothing but static. We got to the stop sign at the end of Main Street. Then we turned left – the wrong way.

I banged on the back of Kyle's seat. 'Hey! Where you going?'

Charlie grabbed my arm, bent it back.

'You've got to take me back,' I shouted, trying to pull away. 'My mom's going to get worried.'

'Your mom?' Kyle turned around so fast I thought he was going to jump over the seat and slap me. 'You think your mom don't know what's going on?' he shouted. 'You think your mom ain't the one who wants us to teach you a lesson?' He looked over at Charlie. 'Her *mom*. Jesus.'

Everybody laughed, like my mom was some kind of joke.

I slumped down, folded my arms, bit my mouth shut. Don't cry, I told myself. Whatever you do, don't cry.

I couldn't tell how far we were driving or how long it took. I tried counting off minutes, like Hansel and Gretel's trail of crumbs, but I lost track because other thoughts kept crowding my head, swirling like Tilt-a-Whirls, red and out of control. Outside of me things moved fast too – the car, the trees, the utility poles whooshing past in the headlights' spill.

Charlie shifted his weight, edged his right leg a little closer. I twisted my body towards the other side. I stared out the side window into the black night, trying to imagine myself someplace else. Lying in the sun. Skiing down a mountain.

Keep calm, I told myself. Keep breathing. Don't worry about the road speeding by. Think of something nice – puppies and flowers.

Thinking didn't work.

The wrong things kept popping into my head. Not nice thoughts, but bad ones, worse places, not better. I pictured us driving off the main highway and down a bumpy narrow-rut road. I felt Kyle and Charlie pulling me out of the car and dragging me into the forest. I smelled dirt and rotten leaves, pictured shovels and pick-axes – digging my own grave.

We drove and drove. I peeked at the side mirror. Tail lights reflected on blacktop, then gravel, back to blacktop again. Every turn, every dip in the road I thought would be the last one, the one before they marched me into the woods and made me kneel down, before they put the blindfold on me or the bag over my head.

Finally, the car slowed down.

This is it, I thought. The final turn-off.

Charlie grabbed me with his left arm, pinned my shoulders against the back of the seat, like he thought I was going to make a run for it, or try to hurl myself through the door while the car was still moving.

'The hell is that?' Kyle shouted.

The guys in the back leaned forward to look out through the windshield. I saw it too – a tall shape in the road. At first I thought it was an animal, but what animal would move like that, jump up and down like it was trying to stop us? What animal would be wearing a red T-shirt? What animal would have dyed blonde hair?

It was a boy.

'You're gonna hit him, man.'

Was the boy crazy? Why didn't he move? His arms were folded in front of his body like that was going to shield him from the car. His eyes were closed, like he was waiting for impact.

I closed my eyes too. In a second, the boy was going to come hurtling through the windshield between Kyle and the driver. He was going to smash into the backseat, crush me to death.

The driver slammed on the brakes. The car swerved, away from the boy, and span around, out of control, faster and faster. The skinny kid ended up on the floor and fat Charlie's body rammed into my side. I got thrown closer to the door. I held onto the armrest and braced myself with my head between my arms, screaming my head off, waiting to be flung out the door and onto the blacktop, or for the car to flip upside down and burst into flames.

PETER

The car skidded away from him, turning round and round like one of those funfair teacup rides. Peter ran onto the gravel shoulder and watched until the car came to a standstill on the edge of the road, still upright but facing sideways. The engine was running and the lights were on, illuminating a deep, narrow ditch.

Inside the car, one of the passengers moved. Something told him – instinct, not Mum this time – that he had to get out of there. Whoever was in the car had just tried to run him over. He had to go – now. He staggered backwards, keeping his eye on the car, afraid to turn his back on it. As the soft shoulder gave way to muddy earth, he skidded down into a drainage ditch, landing face front on the wet ground.

One of the car doors opened. A clumsy shadow tumbled out. He held his breath. Would they see him? He wanted to get up and run, but staying here, clutching his holdall, ducking behind it, was safer –

he could see them, but they couldn't see him.

The shadow scrambled to the middle of the road, stumbled toward him in the dark. As it got closer, he could hear its breath – frantic, terrified gasps. It tripped into the ditch and he saw that it was not an *it*, but a she – a girl, the same age as him, younger even, fourteen, at the oldest. She was flat on the ground, like him, clinging to the wet grass, covering her face, trying not to move.

On the highway, men were climbing out of the car. One guy hopped back and forth, trying to put weight on an injured leg. Another one shouted, 'Etta? Where are you?'

Etta. That must be the girl.

'Hey,' Peter whispered. 'Over here.'

She turned her head slightly. 'Oh, God,' she whimpered. 'Are you with them?'

'No. I was just hitchhiking. They nearly—'

'So that was *you*.'

She didn't say any more. She looked up at the men who were huddled around the car, standing in front of the steaming bonnet, looking back towards the woods, pointing.

She didn't budge. Neither did Peter. It seemed easier, somehow, staying still, waiting for sleep, or for morning, or for the men in the car to find them.

'No, Peter.' That voice in his head. 'You've got to move.'

He shook himself, grabbed his bag. 'We can't just stay here. They'll come looking.'

The girl lifted her face, slithered sideways, closer to him.

'Where can we go?' He could see her eyes, hollow and dazed, ringed in black make-up.

'I know a place,' he said. 'A cabin at Yellow Lake.'

'Where's that?' the girl asked.

'Not far.'

He moved up onto his hands and knees, hooked the holdall straps over his shoulders. The muddy soil squelched between his fingers. They'd have to stay low, crawl to the edge of the woods, before they could make a run for it. A few seconds later, the girl followed him. Peter stopped, waited until they were side by side.

'Don't worry,' he whispered. 'Once we get to the cabin, we'll be safe.'

They crawled towards the forest like clumsy animals. When they got to the top of the ditch, they edged past the first row of trees and shouldered through dense undergrowth. Peter could hear the girl – Etta – beside him. Her breath sounded like his – heaving with effort, but shallow with fear.

They inched forwards until the brambles and tree roots became too dense to push aside. They couldn't have gone very far. It felt like miles – Peter's arms ached, his face and hands burned from the stings of tiny cuts – but it was probably just a few hundred meters. He turned to the girl. Her muddy, matted hair hung down across her face like clumps of seaweed. Her eyes were clearer, though, Peter thought – more determined, less terrified.

'All right?' he whispered.

'Yeah. I'm OK.'

'Would you like to rest here for a while or do you want to keep moving?'

Behind them, a twig snapped. Without speaking, without even looking at each other, he and the girl scrambled onto their feet and took off into the forest, dodging trees, ducking under thick branches. Peter imagined the men behind them – hacking through the scrub with machetes, massive hunting rifles strapped to their backs, waiting for just the right moment when they could stop, take aim, pick them off – first the girl, then him.

But he didn't turn around. He kept going –

tripping, falling, not seeing, not daring to stop, even for a second. He put his hand out for balance and he felt something touch it, hold it, squeeze it – the girl's hand! He squeezed it back. It was strange how he felt stronger, braver, joined to her like this.

'Come on,' he whispered, and they seemed to pick up speed – tramping through the undergrowth, jumping over the roots. His shoes were soaking wet, caked in dirt and slime. His legs ached. His heart was beating so fast he thought his chest would explode. But the girl tightened her grip on his hand, like a silent message – *don't stop, don't stop* – so they trudged on in silence, until the forest got so dense that the trees looked like charcoal smudges on a huge black canvas. . .

Peter stopped. Maybe it was the exhaustion, maybe it was that darkness before the dawn thing, but he couldn't make any sense of where he was any more. Were they moving away from the road? Were they getting nearer to the cabin at all? The forest was a maze, and they'd reached the center – he hoped – but would they ever get back out?

The girl let go of his hand. 'What's the matter?' she panted.

'Nothing,' Peter said, 'it's just. . .'

He felt dizzy. He could hardly see.

'Do you think we've lost them?'

'Dunno,' he said. He crouched down and tied his shoelaces as slowly as he could. He needed to steady himself. They were both out of breath. His lungs were burning. Something rustled in the undergrowth again. It was just a fox or a squirrel scuffling through the dried leaves – Peter *knew* that – but the girl let out a little cry and they were off again, stumbling straight into the darkness like a pair of startled deer. Soon his chest was straining and his legs felt as if they were about to seize up completely. He could hear Etta, just behind him – panting, tripping up, nearly falling.

'You OK?' he whispered. He turned back to Etta, saw a tiny shrug of her shoulders. He glimpsed the mucky curtain of hair that covered her face. He waited for her to say something, but she didn't. It was odd, that – odd for a Yank, anyway. Most Americans he'd met liked talking, so what had made her so quiet?

They were walking now – a slow, silent trudge. Breathing was easier – he took in deep gulps of the cool night air. His vision got sharper. He squinted through the trees for a glimpse of something he recognized – a glimmer of lake, lights from a cabin window, footsteps on a trodden-down path.

It felt safer, too, as if the men in the car had got lost and given up. Or had never even *tried* to find them – that was a possibility, wasn't it? Maybe when he and Etta had disappeared into the woods, the men had stood by the side of the road and waved them goodbye.

'Wait,' Etta said.

He stopped. Listened. What was it? He couldn't hear anything dodgy – just chirping crickets, flitting birds, whining insects.

'I. . .' The girl's voice was a tiny croak. What the hell was the matter? 'Um . . . I gotta go pee.'

Oh, God.

'S . . . sorry,' he stammered, feeling heat rising up his neck, warming his cheeks. 'I'll wait here, OK? You go, you just. . .'

It felt strange, talking to her, especially about something embarrassing like having to piss. His voice was odd in this place, too – posh, as though he should be wearing a dinner jacket or carrying a riding crop.

'I'm gonna go behind a tree,' the girl said.

'Fine.'

It was pitch dark, and he was standing ten feet in front of her, facing the opposite direction. Still, he closed his eyes and covered his face with his hands.

He heard rustling leaves, then the sound of her peeing – like a rushing stream, though he tried not to listen – then more rustling, then nothing.

He waited a few minutes. What was taking so long? He knew girls took forever in the loo, but that was for make-up and stuff, for admiring themselves, wasn't it?

'Right then,' he said, in a clipped voice that reminded him of his father's. 'Maybe we should get moving.'

The girl didn't answer.

'Etta?'

Slowly, the girl came out from behind the tree. As she got closer, and he could see her properly, he noticed how small she was, how young she looked, how fragile she seemed. The black make-up around her eyes had dripped down her pale face like two tiny coal rivers. She was shivering in thin, ripped jeans and a flimsy yellow vest top. She stopped a few feet away from him – her arms wrapped around her body – as if she didn't dare get too close.

'Those men didn't hurt you, did they?' he asked, and straight away he regretted his words, straight away he willed her to say no, she was fine, she'd just got out of that car to stretch her legs, she'd never been in any kind of trouble, it was just the accident that had made her temporarily confused and now she should really be getting back to her nice, normal life.

'I'm OK,' she muttered, her eyes on the ground, as if she couldn't bear to look at him. Then she started to tremble. Her head shook first, then her body. Soon she was shuddering all over, letting out a rumble of choking sobs and tears.

Peter stood beside her, useless. What was he meant to do? Put his arms around her? Hold her? Maybe he should feed her some line about how things weren't so bad, how everything would be all right – every cloud has a silver lining, bollocks like that.

'Don't worry, Etta,' he said. 'We'll get you home soon.'

The crying got louder.

'Do you have a cell phone?' That was good – something practical, at least. 'Should we call your family?'

The sobbing got worse, the shuddering and shaking got so violent that she collapsed onto the ground, and curled up into a little ball.

'Sorry,' he muttered. *Sorry?* How weak was that?

He sat down next to her, took the holdall off his back. What else could he do? Nothing. Just sit. Keep an eye on her, make sure that she wasn't having a seizure or something. Maybe that was it, he thought. Maybe he hadn't upset her at all, maybe she was epileptic. He knew what to do if that was the case – put something in her mouth, a comb or a ruler, so she wouldn't swallow her tongue. *No*, he remembered. That was just a story – complete rubbish, like that if you crossed your eyes too many times they stayed that way.

While he was thinking these things, he started smoothing her hair. He hadn't meant to touch her, and when he realized what he was doing, he wanted to pull his hand back. It seemed to be having an effect, though. Her sobs had shrunk to gentle whimpering. Her breathing was more regular – deeper, calmer. He kept smoothing and petting, imagining that the back of her head was his neighbor's cat, the fidgety one that didn't like anybody stroking it except him. See? He wasn't so bad. Cats liked him, and everyone knew how fussy they were.

At last the girl was quiet and the crackling, hissing sounds of the summer night smothered his random thoughts. Peter let his hand rest on her head for a moment, then carefully took it away. He unzipped the holdall, reached into it, rummaged around for something she could wear. He pulled out a plaid shirt – heavy flannel, an old proper work shirt he'd bought at Oxfam – and put it around her shoulders like a blanket.

The girl sat up, cross-legged like him. She leaned closer to him, trying to make out the features on his face.

'It's hard to see,' she said.

'Sorry.' Another apology. As if the darkness, too, were his fault. 'My name's Peter. Peter Lawrence. I'm from England.'

'I didn't think you were from Welmer.' The girl laughed. That was something.

'The cabin. It's my mum's place. She's a Yank. *Was.* An American, I mean. I was on my way there when you . . . when your . . . sorry . . . when that car stopped.'

The girl was struggling to get her arms into the sleeves of his plaid shirt, so he held it up for her, the way his dad used to help Mum on with her coat.

'Is it far?' the girl asked. 'This cabin?'

'I don't know, actually. I thought I was getting close when you. . .' Why did he stumble on the words, why was it so difficult for him to say what had happened? Why was he sounding so mealy-mouthed, so English, so much like his dad?

'When I *escaped*?'

'Yes.'

'From those *bastards*?'

'Yes.' He knew he should say something else – tell a joke, maybe, or offer 'validation', as Mum called it, not that he knew what that meant.

It was no use – all he had to offer her were some wonky directions and out-of-date travel information.

'If we could find the road again, it might be a couple of miles. If we keep going through the woods, it might be closer, but we're lost now, so. . .'

'So we're probably screwed.'

'Yeah,' he said without thinking, 'although the word I was thinking of was a lot worse than "screwed".'

At first there was silence – forest sounds, bugs and things – but then Etta laughed again, an easy sound, not forced, not something she was doing because she wanted to be polite or to cover up her embarrassment at his lame attempt at humour. She laughed because she got the joke. She laughed because what he'd said was actually funny.

'Right then,' he said, and his dad's brisk, authoritative tone sounded right for a change. 'Are you ready?'

He got up and stood over her, stretching out his hand to help. As she took it, he gently pulled her up so that she was standing beside him.

'Let's keep going this way, and see if we run into something I recognize.'

They moved forwards, deeper and deeper into the woods, stumbling occasionally, but what did that matter? The girl – Etta, he thought, her name is Etta – kept hold of his hand, and he felt that strength again. With every step they took, they were getting closer to the cabin. Peter was sure of it now – he could feel it, drawing them towards it like a magnet. He looked up at the sky. There, through the canopy of trees, bright stars studded the darkness like a trail of tiny lights.

JONAH

A strange noise woke him. He'd heard it before but wasn't sure yet what it was. A fox? A heron? Maybe a distant cabin owner's baby had woken up. In the middle of the night, sounds traveled a long way. No, it was a fox, most likely, barking out a high-pitched warning to her cubs.

For the first time since he'd finished the wigwam, Jonah couldn't sleep. The harsh shrieking that woke him went quiet after a while, but other things – restless, invasive thoughts – wouldn't leave him alone.

At first he thought it was just the hunger, the haunting memories of warm food – a restaurant where he'd eaten with his father once. It was a diner with steamed-up windows. The waitresses were all old, gray-haired ladies with white waitress uniforms and gnarly, blue-veined hands. He and his dad had driven miles and miles from Minneapolis – Jonah didn't know why. But he remembered the food – the old waitress called it a hot beef sandwich. Perfect orbs of steaming mashed potatoes nestled between two huge triangles of roast beef on white bread, smothered – the whole plate – with hot, brown gravy.

That was the last time he'd seen his dad, before he started high school, at the end of middle school when he was about twelve or thirteen. His dad had picked him up from school. He'd stood waiting outside the chain-link playground fence, alone. None of the other parents were waiting – that all finished at the end of grade school. You either walked home alone or you took a bus. His dad was smoking – that wasn't good. He looked confused, out of place, as though he wasn't sure if he was at the right school. Jonah saw Mrs Murphy, who was on after-school rota, pointing at him, whispering something to Mr Cornell, the assistant principal.

Jonah hadn't been expecting his dad, so he wasn't sure what to do. He'd been taught, over and over, not to go with strangers, to report any suspicious-looking people. Did his dad fit that description? It had been a year at least since he'd last seen him. He looked raggedy, with torn jeans and a thin, dirty-looking corduroy jacket that couldn't have kept him warm enough, not on a cold November afternoon.

Mr Cornell started pressing numbers on his cell phone, all the while looking at Jonah's dad, as though if he took his eye off him for a minute he'd abduct someone or pull out a gun.

Jonah raced to his side. 'It's OK. That's my dad.'

The look Mr Cornell gave him was one of complete bewilderment. Who's this kid, he seemed to be asking himself.

'I'm Jonah Campbell. In the eighth grade. Mrs Benson's class.'

Mr Cornell's face registered a little recognition.

'That's my dad. Don't call the police.'

Mr. Cornell's face scrunched up. 'He doesn't *look* like your dad.'

Jonah understood. Indian-looking kid, white dad. Of course it didn't make sense to Mr Cornell.

'Well, he is.'

It didn't make sense to Jonah, either. Not just the Indian/white thing. Not just the never-seeing-his-dad thing. It was his mother's silence on the subject that he *really* couldn't figure out.

His mom was a big-mouth, always trumpeting on about something – how kids today didn't know the meaning of work, how President Bush should have been hauled up in front the Court of Human Rights, whatever that was, how building a new sports stadium in downtown Minneapolis was wasting millions of dollars while people in the Cities were still living on the breadline. It was always something with his mother, but it was never about his dad.

It had been a good dinner, though. So delicious that Jonah had had to fight to keep himself from licking the plate. When they were finished, his dad ordered two slices of lemon meringue pie. It arrived in an instant – a huge slab of neon yellow goo topped with a wobbly white crust that was dotted with droplets that looked like beads of sweat. Jonah could hardly bear to eat it, but his dad needed fattening up, so he kept eating, hoping his dad would too.

Three years had gone by since that weird, silent lunch. Jonah turned over on his mat and inched his body away from the twig that was poking him from underneath the thin cloth. He shouldn't have let himself start thinking about food again, about how he'd kill for just one bite of that gross, sweaty meringue.

He pulled the sheet up to his chest. Thinking about his father, that was another thing. When he was younger he'd lie awake, like this, thinking of all the things he should have said on that last meeting. The usual things like, 'I love you Dad' or, 'I miss you.' Now Jonah knew those words didn't mean a thing. How could you miss someone you never spent any time with? How could you love somebody you never really knew?

The sky brightened. It must have been close to 6:00 a.m. Jonah shook his head. Time! Night? Day? What was the difference, living the way he did now? Soon his body would fall into the rhythms of the nature that surrounded him, and his life, his work, would be determined by nothing more than the rising and setting of the sun and moon, and the changes brought on by the advancing autumn.

Still, he wondered how long he'd been here. He rolled over again on his damp mat, counting back, remembering. There was the first day, traveling from Minneapolis, taking the bus down from Duluth, sleeping curled up in the toilet of a wayside rest. There was the second day, stopping in Welmer, getting building supplies at Hardware Hank and food at the supermarket. There was the third day, trying to build the wigwam, failing, going into the cabin to sleep.

He yawned, sleepy again. Third day, fourth day – what did it matter? He needed to think about what he had to do tomorrow – build a cooking fire, make a trap for rabbits, find some shells and feathers to decorate the weapon he was carving from his firewood club.

On the fifth day, on the sixth day. He turned over on his stomach, agitated. He was thinking like a white man again. Words from the Bible – the wrong creation story – were running through his head. What was he doing, worrying about what God created and when?

He closed his eyes, but the thoughts wouldn't leave him alone. *On the sixth day.* Wasn't that today? Was that why the words were gnawing at him? No, he'd been in the forest for over a week.

On the sixth day. What happened on the sixth day? Had God created something really special?

Jonah curled up so his body faced the door. It was getting brighter now. . .

Adam and Eve. That was it! On the sixth day God created people! He got so lonely he made them out of a hunk of clay.

For a second, Jonah felt proud of himself for remembering – and then he realized how stupid that was. God created people. What was so great about that? Maybe God would have been better off on his own.

Jonah was.

Maybe God couldn't handle being alone, but he could.

People. Who needed them, anyway?

Chapter Eight
—
ETTA

It was Peter who kept me going. He pulled me along, propped me against his shoulders. He must have known that if I sat down or took a rest I'd never be able to pick myself up and start moving again.

I was turning out to be a real liability – like one of those stupid girls in horror movies who wear high heels and prom dresses on a hike through the woods, then twist their ankles while running away from axe-wielding zombies.

How far had we walked? Miles, it felt like, blindly, in the dark.

Then slowly, the sky brightened. We could make things out – the trunks of the trees, the ferns and saplings on the ground, all those holes and hollows we'd been stumbling across. Above us, we could see the outlines of branches. And through the trees, in the distance, something shimmered, silvery-blue.

'That's it!' Peter shouted. 'That's Yellow Lake.'

It seemed huge at first, another Lake Superior. As we got closer it shrank, and when we stumbled onto a tiny beach of scrubby sand – our arms covered in scratches, our faces swollen by bashes and bites – it looked like the most perfect thing I'd ever seen. It was oval, not round, too far to swim across, but shallow and safe, like a gray-blue pool. On the far side, a strip of water was reflecting the sunrise, sparkling like a narrow band of diamonds and gold.

I wanted to stop, to pitch a tent, build a fire, live on this beach for the rest of my life – alone, a forgotten castaway.

But I wasn't alone.

Peter slumped down onto the damp sand. He sat cross-legged, like he wanted to stay, too – just soaking up the beauty. At first he looked straight out onto the water, but then I noticed how his head dropped, how his posture slumped, how his body was turned away from me.

He was crying. He tried to hide it, the way boys always do. He buried his face in his arms and made strange sounds, so I'd think he was coughing or had something in his eyes. But there was no mistaking the movement in his shoulders. Funny. Those shoulders had seemed so broad and strong when we were in the woods. Now, hunched over and shaking, they looked so fragile underneath his thin T-shirt, so breakable.

I sat next to him. Should I touch him? He'd touched me when I lost it back there in the woods, and that had been just the right thing to do. But now, in the morning, it might be weird. Now that we could actually see each other, maybe it wouldn't be the same.

I closed my eyes to make the world dark again. It was easier to think that way. The water smelled weedy and green, fresh. The wind shook the clump of tall reeds, making them brush against my face. I listened to the soft lapping of the waves as Peter's sobs got louder and louder. He'd stopped trying to choke what he was feeling. He was really crying, like somebody whose heart was breaking. I had to do something. I couldn't just ignore him. I could feel my own eyes well up again, and I didn't want that.

'Thanks for saving me,' I said.

It came out stupid and girly, like something Mom taught me to say so I could snag myself a boyfriend. 'I mean it, Peter. I don't know what would have happened to me if you hadn't been there last night.' That part was true, anyway, not that it did any good.

The sobs came harder, sharper.

I just kept talking.

'You probably think I'm stupid, probably think I'm some kind of, well, I don't know what' – I *did* know what, but I didn't want to say the word – 'for getting in a car with strangers. But they weren't *exactly* strangers. One of the guys was my mom's boyfriend. *Allegedly*.'

I told him the whole story – about Kyle sniffing around, even when Mom wasn't home, about him coming around with a bunch of men, about the powder in the bags and the money on the counter. I told him things that happened before Kyle came into the picture, too – having to move to Welmer, having to be on my guard all the time in case Mom got herself in too deep with some guy and I ended up being sent to a foster home.

Peter seemed to be listening. His body was still, but he nodded his head like he understood.

'I just wanted you to know. So you wouldn't think I was some kind of—'

'I didn't think that, not for a minute.' He shifted his body in the sand so that he was staring straight out into the lake, same as me. 'I knew it wasn't your fault.'

I don't know how long we sat there, not talking, just listening and looking out. The sun rose over the tops of the trees behind us, so I took off the heavy shirt he'd given me. He slipped out of his shoes and pulled his socks off, carefully putting the right sock into each shoe, then setting them neatly on top of his duffle bag. He stood up, rolled his jeans to his knees and walked into the water, peering along the shoreline. I leaned back into the sand and let the sun sink into my skin.

I knew he was with me, but I didn't feel like I had to say anything or do anything, or even look at him – not if I didn't want to. And if he didn't want to, he didn't have to say anything, either. If he didn't want to tell me why he got so upset, that was OK too.

'Right then.'

This made me laugh. I couldn't help it. The way he sounded like somebody out of an old black-and-white movie on TV, a man wearing a safari outfit with one of those funny helmets. I'd never met a real English person. Did they all talk like that?

'What?'

'"Right then." The way you said it. It sounded funny to me.'

'Oh,' he said quietly. I looked up at him, worried for a second that I'd hurt his feelings. 'Right then.'

This time we both laughed.

He came back to the shore and dried his feet off with a towel he had in his bag. I sat up and bent over the lake. Luckily it was too wavy to act like a mirror, so I didn't have to see what I looked like. I cupped my hands to splash water on my face and run some through my hair. I kept on and on, splashing and splashing. When my hair was completely soaked, Peter handed me the towel. I dried myself, wiped my face clean.

'Is that OK?' I asked

He smiled at me. I noticed his eyes then – pale blue, like opals. 'You look lovely,' he said.

Lovely. That was good, wasn't it? That meant he thought I looked nice?

I handed him back the towel and the shirt and he folded them up and put them away. I realized then that I didn't want to be alone. It was good to have a helper. Not just for folding clothes more neatly than I'd ever seen it done, not just for guiding me through the forest on a black night. Not for protecting me. Just for being there. It was good to have a friend like Peter – lovely, in fact.

JONAH

It was the next morning, and everything was as it should be. He'd almost forgotten about those stupid white kids from the other night. And the cabin? It was as if it didn't even exist any more.

Jonah went into the woods – naked, except for his underpants and a muslin sling he'd made to gather up his bounty – and collected twigs to use as kindling for his night-time fire. He brought them back into the wigwam and checked on the logs that he was storing – completely dry! And as he walked down the path towards the lake, something peeked out at him from under a clump of leaves – a flash of brightness. It wasn't shiny, like gold or silver, but it caught his eyes and he stooped down to uncover it.

An eagle feather. Well, it looked like one at least – dark brown, smooth, perfectly tapered. His hands shook as he picked it up and ran his fingers along its edges.

His heart pounded, too. He knew what this meant.

From the time he was a little boy he'd heard the stories. To earn a feather, he needed to do something brave or heroic – save a person's life, or kill an impressive animal. His grandfather had told him that – at least he *thought* it was his grandfather. So many of his memories were vague. Maybe he'd dreamed this scene of a small boy, dark brown eyes wide in wonder, sitting on the lap of a kindly twinkle-eyed elder who wore faded denim and a torn red work shirt. In his memory, his grandfather's thick, gray hair was braided. Jonah had no way of knowing if it actually was, though, because his mother never showed him any pictures, never answered any of his questions. His grandfather was just another missing piece from the fractured story of who he was.

When he got to the water's edge, he added the new feather to his now decorated club, tying it on with an old shoelace he'd found on his journey from the city. Then he laid the weapon carefully on the dry sand, and waded into the cool, shallow water. He squatted down to dig in the wet, sandy lake bottom. Hundreds of tiny silver minnows swirled around his arms and legs like whirlwinds of shimmering metal. Jonah tried to sift out some shells, but it wasn't much of a harvest

– stones, mostly, bits of broken glass, smooth-edged, eroded by the sand.

The sun got hotter, the rays caressing the skin on his curved back like a pair of huge, warm hands. He closed his eyes, combing his fingers through the lake-bed, feeling the cool water beneath him, the warm sun above him, hearing the birds, the rhythmic music of the waves. Then something jarred his senses, jerked his thoughts back to the task at hand. Something hard and rough was underneath the sand, something small, pointed, like the serrated tooth of a northern pike or a sturgeon. He lifted it out. He cleared away the grit that had settled in the tiny ridges of its rough surfaces. Then he saw. It wasn't a tooth. It was made of stone and was the color of dull, cloudy amber. It was a small, carved triangle that could only have been one thing – an arrowhead.

Another sign!

His first instinct was to tell someone, show somebody this amazing treasure. But what could he do? Call his mother? Hike through woods until he'd found another cabin, stand in his underpants and tell the white owner what he'd done?

He looked towards the shore, across the empty lake, and sighed. Maybe someone in the spirit world was sharing in his joy, but there was nobody here he could talk to. Still, wasn't that how he wanted it to be? Solitude – wasn't that why he was here?

He stood up, and the dripping water made his underpants cling to his body like a second skin. He loped onto the beach, and picked up his club. He opened his sling, put his precious new treasure inside it. He stood on the warm sand and stretched, arching his body, nearly touching the sky.

That was when he saw them – two white people, trudging through the trees that grew along the shoreline, pushing back the undergrowth, wading out into the water when the bushes got too thick. They were a hundred or so meters away from him and getting closer to the beach – *his* beach – every second.

He slumped down, hunkering behind a row of scrubby pine trees. He stayed totally still, breathing as quietly as he could. He had to calm down, to think. If he'd seen them, then they'd probably seen him too. But did that matter? No – if he crept away silently, if he climbed up the hill to the wigwam, they wouldn't follow him. Why would they? He hadn't done anything wrong. And if they did follow, he could put his twigs onto the path, hide it by roughing up the smooth bits of grass he'd trodden down. They probably wouldn't even notice that there was a path, not if wasn't black-topped or didn't have railings.

He looked down at his club. He'd carved it to protect himself and his land from white intruders. Hadn't he vowed that the next white people he saw, he would see off, by force, if necessary? He could charge through – not to hurt them, just to scare them, to make them run away.

But these white people weren't the same as the others. Even from a distance, Jonah could tell. They weren't drunk. They weren't swaggering and boasting. They looked as though they'd been awake all night, on some grueling march. They looked hungry – like him – and frightened. The girl seemed as tiny and fragile as a doll. Her flimsy T-shirt was dirty and torn, her jeans were caked in mud. The boy, taller than Jonah, with pale skin and a shock of spiky, dyed-blonde hair, held her hand protectively.

Maybe they were lost. That made sense. Maybe they'd taken a wrong direction somewhere and would turn around as soon as they realized that this wasn't the place they were looking for.

He put down the club – that seemed silly now, a bit of ceremonial overkill – and slipped his sling around his front in order to cover up. He hunkered down. What else could he do? He'd have to wait here, hiding like a trespasser, cowering behind trees.

He fingered the arrowhead in his sling. Some symbol, he thought bitterly. He was back to square one – waiting on the white kids, seeing what they'd do before he could make his next move.

PETER

Peter pushed aside the last line of skinny silver birch tree saplings. He scrambled across the beach, breathless with excitement – it was all he could do to stop himself from turning a cartwheel. Finally – *finally* – they'd made it.

'There.' He pulled Etta along, his fear and exhaustion completely forgotten. 'Up the hill. That's it. That's the cabin.'

He stopped in the sand, nearly toppling over.

He looked up the hill, squinted, shook his head.

What the hell?

The steep, sandy hill had crumbled through erosion, and whatever was standing at the top didn't look anything like he remembered. It didn't even look like a cabin. It was an oversized shack with a scrubby, weedy lawn. The paint was peeling, showing gray wood underneath. Dull brown shutters hung from rusty hinges. The window frames were warped by the harsh weather of hot summers and freezing winters. It looked like it hadn't been lived in for years and years.

'No,' he sputtered. This *couldn't* be the cabin. 'It's not. It's not right.'

Maybe he had the wrong place. He was tired. Maybe he was all muddled up.

'There used to be swings here on the sand. They were a bit rusty and the slide was broken but. . .' Peter dropped his holdall, let go of Etta and waved his arms in the air, pointing to a grassy patch of sand. 'There was a firepit – just a circle of rocks, but you could make a fire and find a twig and roast marshmallows.' He paced along the beach. The lake was getting choppier as the sky clouded over. It bashed against a narrow strip of spongy-looking boards that jutted out of the water before listing to the right, on the verge of collapse.

'And that can't be the dock, can it? *Our* dock was painted white and so solid that we could. . .'

Then he saw. The boathouse that had once stood back from the lake, close to the deep woods, was still there. Its roof had sunk in, though, and it was little more than a pile of shattered timber. Beside this shell was a twisted, rusty tangle of metal that had once upon a time been a swing set.

Peter slumped down on the sand, with Etta watching him. He wished suddenly that she weren't there, that she'd just go away so he could be alone for a minute.

All this way, he thought, all this *bloody* way, just to see *this*. Uncle Ken said he hadn't been keeping the place up, but this was more than just neglect, this was total abandonment.

He felt the tears rise up again. No, he wouldn't allow that. Crying wasn't going to help anything now. It was far too late for tears. He had to go up the hill, go inside the cabin, face the worst.

'Right then.' There, he'd said it again. What a bloody pillock. But at least he had a choice now – to cry or to laugh.

There was a moment – the choppy waves stopped crunching against the sand, the wind stopped rustling the tree leaves, the birds stopped chirping. Peter could feel Etta behind him. He imagined her pretty face, not daring to smile, probably by now not even daring to breathe.

He stayed still, facing away from her. 'When I turn around, which I am going to do at the count of five, you'd better not have even a trace of a smile on your face or I will pick you up and throw you into the lake, fully clothed.'

He turned around, smiling, delighted that Etta was there and that he wasn't alone. It was good to have someone to have a laugh with. Somebody who thought he was, well, amusing at least.

But Etta wasn't smiling. She was stone-faced, wearing a still, mask-like expression, her eyes wide. She was staring beyond the beach, looking into the woods and undergrowth on the other side, where something was crunching and shuffling, getting louder as it got closer to them.

'Shit.'

'Kyle,' Etta whispered.

Peter shook his head. No, it didn't sound human – a deer, maybe. He'd seen them here before, taking a drink from the lake. Or it could be a bear. There were bears around. He'd never actually seen one, but they were plentiful now, according to his uncle, and harmless, he thought, unless they were disturbed or needed to protect their young.

He moved closer to Etta and they stepped backwards slowly, not daring to take their eyes off the fringe of the forest.

Wolves, Peter thought. A wolf would be scary.

Etta grabbed his arm, squeezed it.

The creature that came through the woods, kicking away at the underbrush, wasn't a wolf. It was standing upright, but it wasn't one of the men. It was brown-skinned, nearly naked, with long, dark, matted hair. It wore a makeshift rucksack full of twigs and pebbles, and carried a carved, leather-tailed club decorated with feathers and noisy, clicking shells.

It was a boy, no older than Peter and Etta – the strangest-looking kid Peter had ever seen.

Chapter Nine

—
ETTA

It was quiet, except for the lapping waves and the sway of the trees. There we stood – all three of us – stunned and confused, like two castaways in front of a terrified native.

Obviously, the dark haired-kid was nothing to do with Kyle. To begin with, he wasn't wearing any clothes, except some kind of sling across his hips and wet underpants that you could see right through. He might as well have been naked – it was hard not to look.

He was smiling, too, holding his arm out stiffly, like he wanted to shake hands, but in some old-fashioned way.

We didn't shake back, though. We didn't talk. The boy let his hand drop, embarrassed, and pulled the sling lower down across his thighs to cover himself up. Somebody had to break the silence, but all I could think of to say was something lame like, 'We come in peace,' and that didn't seem right. He wasn't an alien, after all, although he looked pretty weird.

Peter let his arm drop from around my shoulder, and picked up his duffle bag.

'That's my cabin,' he said.

The dark boy didn't answer. His face looked blank – maybe he *was* an alien.

'Up on the hill.' Peter pointed to the cabin. He talked really slowly, in case the boy didn't understand. 'The house. It belongs to my family.'

The dark boy thought for a moment, his brows pulled together. He looked up. Nodded. Shrugged. 'That's cool,' he said. 'I'm living in the woods.'

And that was that.

It should have been a bigger moment, like in the movies when people from different cultures meet. There should have been music – trumpets and big drums – blaring from speakers hidden in the woods. Instead, there was another sound – a droning, buzzing noise from across the lake. It was a motorboat, a tiny, far-away speck on the water that was getting bigger, louder, closer.

'Shit,' Peter said. 'They'll see us.'

The dark boy looked out on the water. Then he

turned back to Peter, his eyes wide, and Peter looked at me. It felt like lightning had struck. Suddenly, we all realized the same thing – we all *knew* – none of us wanted anybody else to know we were here.

The dark boy twitched his head, motioned towards the woods. 'Come on,' he said. 'This way.'

He slipped back through the line of trees. Silently, like little kids, Peter and I followed him. Now there were three of us, I thought – Hansel, Gretel and our trusty guide.

PETER

There was only one way to look at it. The Red Indian boy, or whatever he was, was trespassing, plain and simple, squatting on his mother's land, acting as if it belonged to him, not to Peter. And yet, here was Peter, following the stranger onto his own property, like a pathetic sheep. How English. How *very* English.

It didn't take them long to reach the top of the hill. Thanks to the path the boy had trodden, it was easy going, much easier than the tangled miles *he* had led Etta through last night. He resented the new boy's agility and ease, the way he climbed in long-legged bounds, like a leaping deer, while Peter had to force himself to keep moving. The path cut away from the cabin, towards the deeper part of the forest, still part of Peter's land, but virtually ignored by his family and untouched for years. Then they saw it, surrounded by tall trees, shrouded by saplings and ferns and brushy shrubs – a small, domed shelter made of sticks and bark.

'It's a tepee!' Etta squealed.

'No,' the boy said, taking her hand, pulling her towards the clearing, towards the shelter's opening. 'It's a wigwam. A traditional Ojibwe dwelling.' There was pride in his voice as he said it. As well there should be, thought Peter bitterly. The wigwam was neatly made, perfectly shaped, beautiful.

'Look, Peter, a wigwam.'

'Yes. I heard.' Peter's throat was dry; his words came out like pointed jabs. And why did everything he said sound so poncey here, so out of place? They were on *his* family's property, on the land *his* great-grandfather bought years ago with the last of his meager savings and yet he felt like *he* was the one who didn't belong.

'*Boozhoo*,' the boy said. He held out his hand. Peter had no choice but to take it. 'That's Ojibwe for "welcome".'

'*Boozhoo*,' Etta mimicked, smiling at the boy.

'My name's Jonah. I've been living here a while. I don't have anything to offer you. Like, I don't have much food, but I'm planning to set out some traps today and—'

'Traps,' Etta sighed. 'That's so cool.'

Traps, Peter thought. *Cool?* What was she talking about? Some poor fox or rabbit or rat or whatever got impaled on a makeshift torture device and that was cool?

'Trapping is barbaric.' Peter couldn't help himself. He just had to say it. Etta's face fell – good. The Indian boy looked at him, flicking a thick lock of dark hair out of his eyes.

How dare he? thought Peter. How dare he invite them to stay?

'Sorry,' he went on, 'but I just think it's horribly cruel. Hunting, too.' Why was he saying this? He had no feelings about hunting one way or the other. 'Any blood sports. Even fishing.'

The boy, Jonah, smiled. 'You won't be eating much, then. You could try finding some blackberries in the woods, but the bears usually get those first.'

Peter's ears burned and he felt his face getting red – now the boy was taking the piss out of him. 'That's fine,' he said, trying to keep his voice light, trying not to let the resentment creep into his words. 'My uncle's left an entire fridge full of food.'

Suddenly, the need for food and sleep overwhelmed him. So did the desire to be alone. He wanted nothing more than to go into the cabin and to forget about this ridiculous boy in gray Y-fronts and this stupid girl who he'd thought was amazing, but who turned out to be just another stupid . . . stupid. . .

Peter tried out all the nasty words he could use to describe Etta, but none of them fit. None of them were deserved. What had she done wrong? Nothing, except try to be friendly to this new boy, try to show a bit of kindness. And for that he was mentally slagging her off?

'It's been a long night,' he said. 'I'm tired.' Beside him, Etta swayed slightly, as if she were about to collapse. 'There are beds in the cabin.'

She nodded vacantly.

'There's water, too. A shower. And toilet.' He was stating simple facts, uttering simple, truthful words, but it felt as though he were trying to sell her something, as if he were trying to lure her away from the new boy, Jonah, and the amazing things he could do.

'That sounds good.' Etta turned to Jonah, and yawned. 'I'm Etta, by the way, and he's Peter. We're kinda on the run. Guess you must be, too. Maybe we'll see you later.'

That was it. Etta said goodbye and walked with Peter toward the cabin. There was no tussle for her loyalty, no power struggle. When Peter offered her his hand, she took it, as she had in the woods, and let him lead her, once again, to safety.

JONAH

Jonah went back to his chores. What else could he do?

He spent the morning deep in the woods, as far away from the cabin as he could get, gathering twigs and branches, picking berries, rooting out more plants that he could use as medicinal herbs. Then he wandered back down to the water's edge. He looked up and down the shoreline, across to the gentle hummock of forest on the opposite shore. The boat was gone. Good. The lake was empty, clear, calm. He found a spot on the sand that was sheltered by reeds and tall grasses, and sat cross-legged, trying to clear his mind by listening to the sounds around him, the chatter of the squirrels and the airy flaps of swooping birds. He closed his eyes and tried to re-imagine the world, as if he could restore the peace in his heart that had been shattered by the new arrivals.

It was no use. There could be no peace – not now.

He trudged back up to the wigwam, scrunched up some blankets to sit on. He picked up his knife, looked into his sling, took out the new arrowhead. It looked less jewel-like now that it was out of the water. It looked smaller, blunter. Maybe he could sharpen it, shape it into something useful. He held it carelessly in his hand, making random nicks with the knife.

He had to think. He'd been discovered. He'd known it was bound to happen one day, but the suddenness of it was like a blow to his stomach. OK, so it could've been worse. It could've been the sheriff or some rednecks. And the kids seemed nice enough. They were like him – on the run, the girl said. They didn't want anyone to find them either. But that wasn't the point. The point was they'd found *him*. They'd invaded his privacy, his home, his land. And they *weren't* like him. They were white. They were the cancer cells. That was the main thing – they'd only bring trouble.

The knife slipped, slicing through a thin layer of skin on his thumb. The translucent flap hung like the cut bark of a twig, but bleeding and stinging. He put it up to his mouth, sucked as much of the blood out as he could stand, then reached for something to staunch the bleeding, something clean. There was nothing. All his clothes were covered in dirt or sweaty grime and were strewn across the floor of the wigwam where woven mats or skins should have been.

He wrapped his bleeding thumb in a crusty dish-towel he'd taken from the cabin after he'd used it to mop up the white boys' beer. He squeezed it tightly, hoping it would dull the throbbing pain. He wanted to cry, like a big baby. This had all been a stupid mistake. He was a dumb-ass white kid, no different from the others. Maybe it was time to pack up and go back to Minneapolis where he belonged.

He stood up and rummaged through the shirts that lined the floor. A red one, plain, no logo, not too smelly – that would be OK. He picked up his denim shorts, pulled them over his damp underpants. They nearly fell off, resting low on his hipbone. How could he have lost so much weight in less than a week? Maybe going home would be good. There'd be food, anyway.

Still, the unfairness of the discovery made his eyes well up with tears – the sheer bad luck of two kids landing on the beach just as he was coming out of the water. It was too much to bear. If they'd come five minutes earlier he would have seen them before they saw him. If they'd come five minutes later, he would've been back in the wigwam, safe, out of sight. They would have gone into their cabin and fallen asleep. He could have kept out of their way, and nobody would have known any different.

He imagined them now, sleeping peacefully inside, huddled up, safe and secure within their solidly-built walls. They looked sweet, the way he pictured them, covered in warm blankets, as harmless as hibernating bear cubs. If only they were. If only he could trust them.

If, if, if – there were too many ifs. He saw how twitchy the boy looked, how resentful, how likely to pick up the phone, make an anonymous tip-off to the sheriff that somebody was trespassing on 'his' land. He knew what those English were like. Mrs O'Connor had taught him all about them in ninth grade history. They were land-grabbing imperialists, ready to enslave the whole world at the drop of the hat. And anything bad that white Americans did, well, who had they learned it from? Their English ancestors.

The girl had said they were on the run. When he saw them on the beach – dirty, their bare skin scratched and bleeding – they had certainly looked as though they were being hunted by something. But around here, what could that be? Welmer didn't look like the type of town that was in the hands of rival gangs or mafia types. And if they were running away from the police, what could they possibly have done? Not paid for their hamburgers at the local drive in? Stolen candy from the Kwik Trip? They didn't look capable of anything more criminal than overfilling their sodas at Subway.

Subway. Hamburgers. Candy. Inside the cabin was a fridge full of food. That's what the English boy had said.

Once again, Jonah's thoughts led him back to food and his own gnawing hunger. For the first time since he'd fixed the broken door and locked it up, the cabin beckoned to him. It wasn't the security, or the comfort, it was all that food. He remembered the white refrigerator. What treasures would be inside it? Eggs? Bacon? Cheese? His mind wandered further into the kitchen. He opened the fridge door, and took out two eggs. Then he rooted around in the pine cupboards, opened drawers until he'd found a frying pan, some cooking oil, matches to light the stove. He smelled the tang of the oil – no, wait, he'd added some butter – heating. Then he heard the crack of the eggshells, the sharp sizzle as the eggs. . .

'Hey.'

A soft voice jerked him away from his imagined feast. The girl, Etta, was crouching in the doorway.

'I brought you something.'

The mid-morning sun was behind her, lighting up her hair, making it shine like a halo. Jonah knew that it was just the intense brightness that cast her shadow and highlighted the outlines of her body, but Etta looked like an angel – glowing, shimmering.

'Some food. Are you hungry?'

She crawled into the wigwam on her knees, holding out a plate laden with buttered slices of bread and thick hunks of orange cheese. Maybe she *was* an angel, after all. Maybe he'd died or something, drowned in the lake, got beaten to death by those white boys. Maybe the glowing light and the angelic face meant that he was in heaven.

That was what it felt like. That was the only way he could describe it.

Chapter Ten

ETTA

OK, so I thought he was cute.

After we'd gone into the cabin, I couldn't sleep. It was weird being so tired but not being able to close my eyes. They hurt when I did, so it was better to keep them open.

It might have been the light coming through the big window. Closing the thin cotton curtains hadn't made it much darker, but Peter said this room was better because it had its own bathroom, like a hotel room. I tried pulling the blanket over my head – that just made the whole world pink, not dark.

In this pink world, there was a tiny toy train, like one I'd seen in a toy store once, going around a little track way up on the ceiling, only this train was all my thinking about what had happened in the last twenty-four hours.

Mom.

I thought I knew her, at least enough to know that there was a limit to what she would and wouldn't do. I mean, she might try to fiddle things, like stuff tips down her bra so she wouldn't have to claim them for income tax, but she'd never actually steal. Or she might threaten to leave. Back when my brothers were in high school she'd do that about every month or so, with me crying in the corner and Cole looking ashamed for something he'd done and Jesse just pissed off because he'd heard it all so many times before. But she'd never actually take off. And we *knew* she never would. We knew she'd stomp out, close the door, wait for about five minutes, long enough to have a quick smoke, then come back in with a funny story about how the lady next door was using a vacuum cleaner to get leaves off her sidewalk.

So what the hell had happened now, with Kyle? Had she finally cracked? She couldn't have known what he was going to do, could she? All that stuff he'd said about it being her idea, that 'teaching you a lesson' crap – he had to be lying.

Still, if she was dumb enough to go out with Kyle in the first place, to let him into our house, into her bedroom, she could have been dumb enough to—

No. *No.*

Then why couldn't I stop imagining Mom and Kyle having a party, celebrating that I was gone? There'd be a store-bought cake, specially decorated for the occasion. Charlie and that weasel kid from the car would be there, chugalugging cans of beer, spraying the inside of the trailer with foam or bubbles from cheap sparkling wine. Mom would be on the counter, dancing in denim cut-offs and a halter top and leopard skin sandals – the belle of the ball, the queen of all she surveyed.

No. That wouldn't happen. Don't think that.

Well, she must have known about that stuff in the kitchen at least – the powder, the money.

No. Don't be stupid. She couldn't have known about *any* of this.

Peter had said there was a phone in the cabin. There was no way I was going to call her, not now. I didn't dare, not with the way things were. What if I found the worst?

As for Jesse and Cole – I didn't have their phone numbers, and they were too clueless to go online. My own brothers, and I didn't even know what states they were living in. Some family we were.

Of course there was Grandpa. If I called Grandpa, I knew what he'd do – get in his car straight away.

As soon as he got the call he'd be gone, and nothing would stop him from coming to get me – nothing or nobody, not even Grandma.

I imagined the Duchess waiting in the doorway after Grandpa picked me up. Her face would be fixed into a smile, like she'd painted it on with lipstick to hide the real expression underneath. She'd be wiping her bony hands on a dish-towel, so I'd know how much hassle I was causing.

I'd just have to take care of myself. I'd be all right. Peter had this cabin. There was a bedroom, a bathroom, a kitchen – what more could I want? There was food, he'd said, plenty of food.

God, I was hungry.

The room where Peter was asleep was just off the kitchen, in a little alcove set away from the main living room of the cabin. I crept into the kitchen and slowly opened the fridge door in case it creaked. I peered inside. Nothing, except for some moldy cheese and two cracked eggs that looked fossilised. There was a nasty smell – something that could have been lettuce leaves was lying dead in the bottom of the crisper. And the freezer was iced over, with mounds of snowy particles hiding ice cube trays and an empty waffle box. No feast in the fridge, then. So where was this huge stock of groceries that Peter had told Jonah about?

The cupboards were almost bare too. There were cans of tomatoes and tuna, saltine crackers, two boxes of macaroni and cheese mix, a plastic container of stale corn flakes. And for dessert? Three boxes of pudding mix and a bag of petrified marshmallows.

I wanted to cry.

Still, there was the food that Peter had brought from town, sitting on the counter in a paper bag – a big loaf of white bread, some Velveeta cheese, a package of Lipton tea bags, half a gallon of milk and two tiny green apples. I put the milk in the fridge, made myself a sandwich and an extra for Peter, the way I used to make extra when Jesse and Cole were at home.

I cut the sandwiches into little diagonals, thinking about the best way to use up the milk. That macaroni and cheese supper mix would probably call for milk. I could use milk in the pudding mix, too. Macaroni and cheese, chocolate pudding – that would make a decent meal. And I could do something with the tuna and tomatoes – save some of the macaroni and have a kind of pasta thing. I could even melt the marshmallows, mix some cornflakes into them to make a nice dessert.

Things weren't so bad, after all. I found a set of pretty, old-fashioned yellow dishes in a cupboard. I put Peter's sandwich on a plate, and wrapped it in aluminum foil from one of the drawers. I went to the alcove doorway and listened in. I could hear him breathing – deep, steady, just a little bit of a buzzing snore. He'd like that – waking up to a plate of food.

Suddenly, I was Betty Crocker, Suzy Homemaker and Mom on one of her cooking benders, all rolled into one.

'The ghost of Grandma Hanson,' Mom called it, after some Norwegian ancestor of hers. The ghost would strike every year, usually around Christmas, and turn Mom into a good housewife against her will, making her take out the old, crusty cookbooks that were stashed away in the back of the cupboard, forcing her to buy cheap women's magazines that were on display at the supermarket checkout.

Then, for maybe a week, she'd cook and clean, trying out the magazine tips that involved polishing with lemon juice and vinegar. She'd bake stuff and freeze it – casseroles using Poppin-fresh dough and Tater Tots, weird concoctions that ended up tasting like over-salted cardboard.

This would go on until she tried something tricky

that wasn't based on a mix – maybe a soufflé, or pastry from scratch. Then it would all go wrong, so that by the time the ghost finally left her, there'd be dishes piled up in the sink and hunks of dough would be left on the countertop and spattered on the stove. The kitchen would stay that way, batter hardening like concrete, until, a week later, she'd pay me five bucks to chip everything off with a metal scraper.

Maybe it was the ghost of Grandma Hanson who made me think of the boy outside, made me wonder if he was as hungry as me.

I felt guilty worrying about him, though. This was Peter's place, Peter's really special place, and this other kid was trespassing. Peter hadn't called it that, he hadn't said anything, but he was upset about it. It was in his eyes, the way they flashed and twitched.

Peter wouldn't want me sharing our food with the Indian boy.

But still, it didn't seem right – that kid out there starving, while we were in here with enough food. We'd have to share. We couldn't just leave him alone, could we?

PETER

The sound of bells woke him. Where was he? Back in England? No. Italy? On holiday?

He pulled off his covers and it came back to him. He was at the cabin. The bell he was hearing was from that old-fashioned dial phone that hung on the kitchen wall.

The telephone. Bollocks!

'Hey Pete!'

Uncle Kenneth. Thank God. Not Peter's dad. Ken's voice sounded rough and staticky, as if it were a thousand miles away, at the end of a long, clogged wire.

'You were gonna call me.'

Peter wondered how long he'd been asleep. It was still daylight, so not too long. He looked at the clock on the cooker – almost noon.

'Yeah, sorry about that,' he said, yawning.

'Well, I hope everything's still in one piece up there.'

Ken's voice sounded normal, affable, upbeat – the way the sentence tilted up at the end let Peter know it was a question, but that he was only interested, not suspicious.

'Everything's fine, Ken. I had a hard time getting here, though.' He told part of the story – the closed road, the long walk, the exhaustion, the dawn arrival. He didn't say anything about a kidnapped girl or an Indian boy in a wigwam.

He noticed the sandwich on the table. It looked like a present, wrapped in kitchen foil, neatly tucked in at the edges. All it was missing was the bow. Etta must have done that.

'Say, yeah, you know, I got a call from your dad.'

'Oh, really?'

He tried to sound like his uncle – casual, not bothered. To make himself sound even more distracted, he opened the cupboard that was next to the phone, put his free hand in and started rummaging in the contents – instant iced tea mix, a bag of sugar in a sealed plastic container. Was his uncle doing the same thing – putting on an act?

Peter opened the sugar container. 'I hope everything's OK with him.'

'Well. . .' There was a slight hesitation. It was as

if he were trying to put together the right chain of words, to piece things together in his mind.

'It was on the answering machine, so I haven't actually talked to him. Just a message, but it was kinda weird, like, "Is he with you?" I didn't quite get what he meant.'

'That *is* odd.' Peter was casual again, as if he hadn't the foggiest idea what his dad could have meant. He tried to sound impatient, too – didn't his uncle know he had things to sort out here? The sugar container was crawling with black ants, for God's sake.

'Just thought it was kinda, well, like you said. Odd. Like he didn't know where you were.'

Then Peter went for decisive, slamming shut the cupboard door. 'He was probably worried that I hadn't got here yet. I told him I'd call straight away, but I fell asleep. I was just about to call him now, that is, if you don't mind.'

There was silence from the other end. The phone line crackled as if it were getting congested with a traffic jam of unspoken words – Peter's lies, Uncle Kenneth's unasked questions.

'You sure everything's OK?'

'Of course.' He gave a weak laugh – a nice touch. 'I just wish I'd picked up a few more things at the shop in town. It's a long walk in.'

'You know, if you call the store Duane'll deliver for you. Tell him to put it on my account.'

And that was that, except for a few more 'yeps' and 'all rights' and the final seal of trust and approval – Uncle Ken saying 'you bet' before putting down the phone.

Peter felt sick, a raw, gurgling ache in the pit of his stomach. His uncle knew something was up. They were both crap liars. He might as well get on the phone, call his uncle, his dad, tell the whole world where he was, what he'd done, wait to be collected by some county social worker, to get bundled onto a plane back to England, and met by his father's stern jaw fixed in position.

'Do you know what this has cost me – your little *escapade?*' He heard his father's clenched-teeth words, hissing like venom from the mouth of a snake. Dad would pause before he used the word 'escapade' to add extra effect, to make it sound as though he were searching for just the right word, even though he would've had his lines all figured out ahead of time, the way he always did.

Arrogant git.

Peter took the phone off the hook and set the

receiver down on the worktop, half tempted to cut the twisted cord with a knife. If Uncle Ken called back, he'd think he was on the phone to Dad. If his dad phoned and couldn't get through, that was tough.

He took a bite of the sandwich Etta had left on the table. Not bad. Maybe it was because someone else had made it, but the bread tasted softer, fresher than it had yesterday. Maybe it was the dampness in the air. He put it down. He'd wait until Etta had hers. It was only polite.

He went back to his room and straightened the bed. When he was little, this had been his favorite room. Although it was in the center of things, between the kitchen and the main living area, it seemed like a hiding place. Everything in it was child-sized. The single bed that always had – still had – a white candlewick spread with nubs that he twiddled with his fingers to help him fall asleep. The tiny window that only a child could get through, or else a small, harmless animal. Bears couldn't get him in this room, or wolves, or giants or robbers. He was safe here – it was like being a baby, cocooned in his mother's arms.

He walked across the living room to the bedroom where Etta would be sleeping. Now that it was lighter, the dirt showed up. There were streaks on the window where months of rain had come lashing down. The floor seemed sticky under his feet. There was a dusty scum on the tables, grimy smudges on the glass-topped desk, as though somebody had made a mess and only half cleaned it up. Soot and the remains of crumbled kindling twigs had been blown across the hearth tiles and had settled in the cobwebs that were spreading in the corners and crevices.

Two small steps and a tiny hallway separated the bedroom from the rest of the house. He trod carefully toward the closed door then knocked gently. Nothing. He should leave her to sleep. She must have gone back to bed after making his sandwich. Still, he wanted to see her, make sure she was OK.

He opened the door a crack. The bathroom door was open, the bathroom light on, the fan humming. The double bed looked empty, but the way the covers were bunched up in the middle, a soft, tube-like hump, he couldn't tell. She was so tiny, she could easily fit in there.

'Etta?'

Then he heard it – through the open bathroom window. Laughter. It was musical and sweet, as though somebody were practicing a scale on a flute.

Etta's laughter, followed by somebody else's – that Indian boy's.

Peter stood still for a while, listening, a spy in his own house.

JONAH

Once, when he was small – he couldn't have been more than four or five – Jonah had had what his mother called a 'little girlfriend'. Sometimes she pronounced it in a high, sing-song, baby voice – *'widdow gewfwend'*. Even then, the mocking way she said things had made him angry.

The girl's name was Melissa and her mother had been a friend of his mom's. He and Melissa would play together in her bedroom while the two mothers sat in the kitchen, drinking coffee or wine, depending on what time of day it was, smoking cigarettes, coughing and cackling.

Melissa's single bed had a white canopy over it, a pink flowered bedspread on top of it and, stashed underneath it, crate-loads of pink toys. Barbie houses, Barbie cars, Care Bears, pink building blocks, My Little Pony coloring books. At the time, Jonah had thought even Melissa's name was pink, the way it reminded him of cotton candy at a fairground, delicate strands of pastel spun sugar, sweet and melty, just like her.

He couldn't remember being anywhere else with her – the park or his apartment – he could only remember that pink room and the way it glowed, and how Melissa had seemed to be what was lighting it up. Her hair was strawberry blonde and she had two dimples either side of her smile, as though somebody had dipped a spoon into her cheeks because they were as soft and smooth as whipped cream.

Looking back, as he did sometimes, especially when he got older and saw Melissa around at school or in the supermarket on Lake Street buying cigarettes with her hard-faced friends, he realized that he must have been in love with her.

What else could it have been? He would have done anything for her. He gave her his candy, he played whatever stupid girl game she wanted to play, dressing her dolls up, dressing *himself* in clothes from her dressing up box – plastic high heels, a white, satiny slip and bra, a shiny patent leather purse to match – so they could play shopping. Even then, he knew that there was something weird about a boy wearing plastic high heels, even then he felt humiliated by what she asked – no, insisted – that he do, but he didn't care. Anything she asked, he would have done it – stolen from his mother, eaten worms, run across Interstate 94 during rush hour, swallowed rat poison.

In the end, what she asked him to do was to draw pictures all over her white flowered wallpaper with black magic markers and pour bright green poster paint onto the new pink wool carpet her mother had just bought. It took weeks for her mother's shrieks to stop ringing in his ears, years for *his* mother to stop blaming him for losing her such a wonderful friend as Melissa's mom.

The girl sitting in his wigwam didn't look anything like Melissa, so why did she make him think of her? This girl's hair, once the sun stopped shining behind it, was matted close to her head as though it hadn't been washed in a week. She fiddled with it, the way girls always did, twisting a greasy strand around her fingers, pulling at the ends, running her fingers through it as if her hand were a comb.

She'd come in a little nervously, poking her head in, stepping through the doorway, following his nodded instructions to sit down on the ground. She looked around at the things that he'd managed to fasten onto the fragile bark walls, admiring them, he thought – pictures he'd printed off from the internet.

A sepia photograph of a huge herd of buffalo, some cave pictures from Mexico or Italy – at least that's what the place sounded like to him. *Altamira.* He'd even tried doing his own straight onto the bark – he'd used a little kid's watercolor set that he'd brought with him – but they looked like green and brown stains, smeared-on snot or puke. He'd get some paper, try again later.

'How long you been here?'

It was just a simple question, but he was so used to questions being loaded, questions from his mother being more like interrogations, that he got paranoid straight away. Did he smell bad, was that what she was getting at? Or was she spying for the English boy, pumping Jonah for information so that they could get him evicted?

'A week.'

'Wow. I thought you'd been here for way longer.'

'I look that bad, eh?'

'No, God, no.'

She laughed, that pretty sound, as if she were singing. 'No worse than me, anyway.'

When they both laughed, their two voices got mixed up together – hers high, his low.

Like music, he thought. A beautiful song.

ETTA

Like I said, Jonah was cute. And mysterious, in a way.

'Different,' my mom would have said, only to her 'different' was never a good thing, it was something weird and hard to understand, maybe even dangerous.

But Jonah wasn't that. He was intense. Not just quiet in the way that Peter was, with words inside him, desperate to come bubbling out, if only he'd let them. With Jonah, there were weren't many words at all. His voice was deep and he hardly opened his mouth when he talked. With Jonah there were feelings, thoughts – so many that it must have caused him pain to actually express them.

That's the way it seemed, anyway, sitting cross-legged opposite him, glancing at his face, trying not to stare. God, he *was* cute – black hair, dark eyes, nut-brown skin – nothing like the normal run-of-the-mill, flabby, white-bread, pizza-faced guys who roamed the streets of Welmer.

Different. Beautiful. Way prettier than me, anyway. Not that *that* was saying much.

'This is nice. Your wigwam, I mean.'

What an idiotic thing to say. Quick, say something else, something smarter. 'It's so sturdy and it's like it . . . belongs here.'

'It does,' he said.

I looked around, as if I was checking it all out again. I put both hands up to my hair, twirled a strand, twisted it tight.

'Your friend still asleep?' Jonah asked.

'Oh, Peter's not my friend,' I stuttered. 'Not like my *boy* friend anyway.'

Why had I said that? The words came out so fast. Suddenly, the wigwam felt hotter, seemed brighter. The sun must have come out from behind the clouds.

'I bet that's not the way he sees it,' Jonah said, the trace of a smile in the corner of his mouth.

'No, no, you've got it all wrong.' I tried not to smile. It didn't feel right, making light of Peter and me, of what we'd been through. 'No, I mean it, we're just friends.'

This was stupid. I didn't need to explain anything to Jonah. Peter didn't need defending.

'He saved my life,' I said.

Jonah smiled, raised his eyes. 'Yeah?'

'Yeah.' I could have told him the whole story then – about Kyle, about the men, about the woods – but I didn't have the energy. It would have to wait.

'So, how long have you guys known each other?

I thought back. Last night. It must have been after midnight when Kyle's car nearly ran Peter over. What time was it now? Noon, maybe. I counted back the hours, touching my fingers to make sure.

'Twelve hours.'

That couldn't be right.

'Not very long, then.'

I counted again, silently. Twelve hours. So much had happened. It was all going so fast.

'Seems longer,' I said.

Jonah nodded, like he understood. It seemed like we'd been here forever. He must have felt that way too.

PETER

It took Peter half an hour to clean the bath out properly. Three years' worth of dead bugs, some old grimy soap scum that had never been rinsed off, a thin layer of rust and limescale – it was disgusting.

He'd put the hot water on first thing, as it said on the instructions written out in Mum's handwriting. Power – check. Hot water heater – check. Pilot light on the furnace and the stove – check. It felt easy, as though he knew exactly what to do, as if that sequence had been encoded into his DNA.

He gave the tub one last rinse and turned the hot faucet on. Out came a rusty spew, like something coughed out of a dying man's lungs. The stream of steaming water cleared in a minute, and Peter ran a capful of bubble bath. He sat on the edge of the bath, listening to the gurgling spray, trying to block the sound of more laughter from outside.

The bubbly bath stuff smelled like something Mum

would've bought – a herbal and woody scent that reminded him not only of her, but of his night in the forest with that girl who was now outside trying to pull an Indian bloke.

Stop it. Why was he thinking these things? The feeling that burned inside him shouldn't have been there, and the fact that it *was* there, clogging his throat, twisting his gut as if he'd just swallowed poison, made him hate himself.

Maybe it was just the exhaustion. Once he was clean again, once he'd had something more to eat, once he could 'take stock' as his father was always doing, he'd be able to figure out a way to get his plan on track again, to get his time here, his life here, sorted.

He had to peel off his clothes, they were so dirty. His shirt hit the floor with a thud, dropping like a chunk of masonry from a building. His hardened shorts skidded down his legs, the belt clanking onto the tiles. He dipped a foot into the bath. It was almost painfully hot – that was good. Slowly, he put both legs in, ankle-deep in the near-scalding water, watching his skin redden as he sat down in a crouch, letting out short gasps of breath like a child cooling down a spoonful of too-hot soup.

Steam rose around him, making the bathroom as

foggy as a primeval swamp. It felt good. Even the hot, wet air seemed to be cleaning him, inside his lungs, into his mouth, his ears. As he breathed in deeply, the air seemed to enter his bloodstream, his heart and his brain, clearing him out, calming him, making him relax, making him feel as lethargic and dopey as he had when he'd smoked that joint with one of his stoner second cousins after Mum's funeral – the only thing that had seemed to dull the misery, dull the anger, dull everything, dull, dull.

He wasn't thinking, really. Definitely not praying or meditating, he was just being warm and getting clean. It was like what happened at his Uncle Ken's condo, only dreamier. Thoughts of Mum – clear, vivid memories – rose up out of the steam and brushed over him like gentle waves, like warm, wet, transparent clouds.

Home. England.

The sound of words.

Not an argument, but sharp, heartfelt words, that seemed to divide his mother and father even as they brought them together. Whenever they talked like this, she became more agitated, brasher, more American with every syllable. His father would take the opposite tack, narrowing his voice to a near whisper that was clipped and precise, as English as could be. Quiet but powerful. Not aggressive, but not giving an inch. On and on they would go, using words that he hadn't understood. *Rapprochement*, what the hell was that? *Realpolitik*? And why were these words coming into his head now?

Then, despite the inevitable slammed doors, despite the tears, the walks to the corner shop and back, they would always end up on the sofa, kissing. At least Mum kissed. His father accepted her kisses, her laughter, her cajolery, her *rapprochement*? Was that what it meant – making up, being friends again? Then the following night, it would be something else, usually accompanied by the clinks of wine bottles, or friends round the candle-lit oak table in the dining room. There'd be laughter and then those words again, getting louder as the night wore on, making it impossible for him to sleep upstairs, but not loud enough for him to totally hear the conversation.

He remembered once going out to the landing to eavesdrop. His mother's voice was a foghorn cutting through the English pleasantries and sophistication. He heard what she was saying – that rapprochement thing again, co-existence, co-operation, rapprochement, conciliation – but he had no context to match what she was saying. This wasn't a story or a speech, it was just words flying out of her mouth like birds, up the stairs in a flutter of wings, into his ear, squawking, feathers flying.

Then he saw her face clearly, as if he were looking into a mirror and it was she, not he, who was reflected back. Her face before she was ill. Her freckles, even on her lips, the ones she hated and complained about every summer when the sun brought them out. The crinkles around her eyes when she laughed, the deepening folds around her mouth, the lines on her forehead that she jokingly threatened to have botoxed. Her eyes, like his, such a pale pastel blue.

Her hair, blonde like his, but wavy – a wiry nest of curls.

Her hair. He'd forgotten about the hair.

Rapprochement. What the hell *was* that?

He must have fallen asleep. When he opened his eyes the water was lukewarm, a horrible dishwater gray. Something had woken him up with a start – the sound of a car door slamming shut.

JONAH

Etta heard it first.

'What's that?'

'What?'

'Like tires.'

Instinctively, she moved away from the entrance flap, edged back toward the forest side of the wigwam. Jonah noticed for the first time the color of her dark eyes – deep blue, like the lapis lazuli earrings his mom always wore. Now they flashed out so much fear, they seemed hot, like shiny pieces of overgrown buckshot.

He opened the flap and peered outside. A car was in the driveway – a banged-up, rusty, white four door. A man got out, slammed the door, leaned against it, lighting a cigarette. He wasn't a cop – thank God – or one of the drunk teenagers. He was older, in his forties maybe, although it was hard to tell because he was so fat. His thin gray T-shirt was stretched over a huge belly, then tucked into faded, low-hanging jeans. He was looking around, taking everything in – the cabin, the driveway.

The woods.

'Who is it?' Etta whimpered in the corner like a lost child or a trapped animal.

'Don't know. Some guys.'

Another door opened and closed. The second man was younger, maybe in his early twenties, with straw-colored hair and a long, skinny face that made him look like a weasel. He was carrying something – a kind of shovel, a pointed garden spade that you'd use for digging or spreading.

'What are they doing?' Etta was curled up in a little ball, her head between her knees, cradling herself. 'Jonah?' Her voice was hoarse, wheezy.

'Nothing. Just looking around. It's OK.'

The fat man waddled towards the front door of the cabin, checking out the driveway, glancing back, as if he wanted to make sure no one followed them in or could see them from the highway. The skinny-faced kid, lighter on his feet, took off the other way, towards the wigwam, towards *them*.

Jonah's heart pounded. Even from a hundred yards away, he could smell bad intentions. Whoever these guys were, whatever they were up to, they weren't the type who took kindly to long-haired Indians hanging out in wigwams with underage white girls. He had to get out of here, before it was too late, for Etta's sake too. A local girl hanging out with a dark-skinned stranger? There was no telling what these yahoos might do.

'Look,' he whispered. 'I'm going to clear out, OK?' Etta's eyes got wider, but she didn't say anything. 'In case they come looking.'

He inched toward the flap of the wigwam and pulled back the flimsy tarpaulin.

'It'll be better if you're all alone.'

Without saying anything else, he slipped through the flap and loped away from the wigwam. Would Etta scream, he wondered. Would she beg him to come back?

No. She was too scared. She wouldn't make a peep.

As he slipped into the deep cover of ferns and brush he tried not to think about the fear in her voice or the burning look on her face. What he was doing was for *her* good too. He'd explain it all later when he got back. She'd understand.

'Hey!' A man's voice – could somebody see him?

'Hey, Charlie!'

Jonah dropped behind a fallen tree and crouched down onto the damp ground. He rubbed his hands into the wet dirt and spat on them to make a muddy paste that he wiped onto his face as camouflage. He looked through the leafy branches that stuck out from the tree. He had a clear view of the driveway, the lawn, the side of the cabin.

The fat man was at the kitchen door. He tried the handle and backed away when it wouldn't open. He looked up at the roof, back at the car that was parked in the driveway. He strolled towards the side of the cabin, closer to the wigwam, and peered through the bedroom window.

From somewhere else in the front yard the other voice called out. 'Still empty, Charlie?'

'Looks like it,' the fat man said.

'Why don't you go inside and check it out?' The other voice – the boy's – sounded louder now, closer. Jonah couldn't see him, though, so he stretched his neck above the cover of branches and leaned over the log, trying not to rustle any leaves.

'Door's locked,' the fat man shouted. 'Thought you guys kicked it in.'

'The boss musta come out and fixed it.'

Jonah ducked back down – the boy was less than

twenty meters away, standing next to the propane gas tank on the edge of the scrubby lawn, taking a piss.

'Why don't we look inside?' he said. 'Must be something worth taking.'

'You heard what the boss told us. That ain't what we're here for.'

When he was finished, the kid picked up his shovel and stepped into the woods. Jonah held his breath. He could hear the boy, walking around, crunching the leaves underfoot. Maybe these guys were gardeners, Jonah thought, or tree surgeons checking for ash borer. That made sense.

Then the weasel started to do something else. Jonah listened – stone and twig scraping against metal, the gentle *thunk* of fresh soil dropping onto the ground.

Digging.

'Everything's checking out, Charlie. Ground's good and soft.'

A few cuts later and the boy stepped back onto the grass, carrying the dirt-covered spade as though he were brandishing a spear. He spat out the cigarette he'd been smoking and trudged back to the car.

Charlie, the fat man, waddled towards the driveway. He was carrying something too. What was it? Jonah hadn't noticed it before – Charlie must've gone back to the car to get it, or maybe he'd been holding it by his side so it was hidden by his enormous belly. Jonah squinted to get a better look. Long and skinny. Metal. Another shovel?

A gun.

Something twisted in the pit of Jonah's stomach.

Charlie moved the gun to his other hand, and Jonah could see it more clearly. It was a shotgun – clunky, heavy-looking, a long barrel with two black holes at the end. Was that the kind of gun that hunters used? Is that what these guys were doing – hunting, looking for squirrels or rabbits? Did they know the place was empty so they thought they'd take some potshots?

Yeah, Jonah thought. Hunters. That was it.

Shooting practice. It had to be.

He took a deep breath. He needed to slow his racing heartbeat, control the pitiful fear that made him want to puke, smooth away his shameful desire to curl up on the ground and cry like a baby.

The weasel-faced boy was back in the car, waiting for the fat man. He leaned on the horn, and the sudden racket set a flock of blackbirds squawking and flapping through the air. Charlie stopped walking, and as soon as the birds were clear of the trees, he turned, looked, lifted his gun and took aim—

Too late. Before he could open fire, the birds scattered, flew out over the cabin, towards the lake.

Charlie opened the back seat and tossed the gun onto the floor of the car. He said something to the boy, stretched the seatbelt over his belly, closed the door, turned on the car's engine.

And then they were gone. Jonah watched the battered car disappear at the end of the long driveway and get swallowed up by the trees that loomed over the main road. The sounds of the woods got louder – insects droned, a pine cone dropped to the forest floor.

Jonah stood up, stepped over the log he'd been hiding behind. Somewhere near the lake, the flock of blackbirds squawked angrily – had they been watching him from their perch high in the trees? Had they seen him slink away from the wigwam and tremble like an old woman at the sight of the white man's gun?

He'd come back to the forest later – after he'd talked to the girl, after explaining himself. He'd find medicine in the earth – healing herbs, powerful plants. He'd build a fire with them, make an offering that might smudge and burn away the stain of what he had just done.

Behind him, a twig snapped, making him jump and gasp. He turned around – waited, watched. It was nothing, *nothing* – just squirrels or chipmunks. As he loped back towards the wigwam, Jonah heard their mocking chatter.

'Some *Anishinaabe* this one is,' they seemed to be saying.

'Frightened white boy,' they seemed to laugh.

ETTA

The quiet was creepy, like one of those stagnant ponds full of nasty garbage just below the surface. There'd be other cars. The men – Charlie and whoever the other guy was – would come back.

I stayed in my snug little burrow at the back. Without Jonah inside, the wigwam looked flimsy. The pictures he had put up were hanging on by thin string. The skinny branches that supported the bark walls looked like they could snap back any second. This was like one of the three little pigs' houses, the one made out of twigs. It would've been safer if I'd stayed in the cabin with Peter. Real wood. Solid walls.

I needed to get into the cabin – the safest place, even if it wasn't made out of bricks – but I didn't dare move. Charlie might be waiting till I let my guard down so that he could pounce on me as soon as I slithered out of my cocoon.

Something rustled outside. Footsteps.

'Etta?'

A few seconds later Jonah came in, hesitating as he opened the door flap. What was he waiting for? Did he think they'd killed me or something? Was he scared my blood-soaked body would be dripping all over his precious wigwam floor? He must have known what those guys were capable of. That's why he ran. Because he *knew*.

In movies or books, when people bail they don't last long. Anyone who's ever seen a monster movie knows the rules – you abandon the kids, you get eaten by a T. rex. You leave the girl with the twisted ankle behind, you get your limbs hacked off with an axe or a chainsaw – it's as simple as that.

Still, Jonah came into the wigwam, like he thought he could snivel his way out of his fate. He sat in the middle of the floor, legs crossed, the same as before, only it wasn't the same.

'What do you think they'd have done if they found us together?' he asked.

I stayed where I was – curled up, at the back of the wigwam, as far away from him as I could get.

'One guy had a gun,' he said. 'Another guy was holding a shovel.'

A gun. A shovel. And they were looking for me.

'What d'you think they'd have done?'

'I know what they'd have done,' I said. '*You* know.'

He leaned over, tried to touch me, a little pat on the arm to show how sorry he felt. He might as well have lashed out with a poisoned tentacle. I pushed him away, backed further into the corner.

'Me and you together?' he said. 'Local white girl, dark-skinned boy? That's why I ran out. I thought you'd be safer on your own.'

'You did, did you?' I said. Those big, dark eyes of his, the ones I'd thought were so awesome – I couldn't even bear to look at them.

'They wouldn't have hurt you. Not on your own, a helpless girl.'

'Is that what you think? Men don't hurt girls.'

'That's not what I meant.'

'You think men like Charlie need a reason?'

He tried to touch me again, like that would make me feel better. Like a gentle rub on the shoulder could wipe away what'd he'd done.

'Sorry, Etta,' he said. His voice sounded funny – choked up. What was he trying now? Tears?

'A gun and a shovel,' I said. 'That's what they had.'

'Please, please, Etta, I just thought. . .'

A gun and a shovel, and he still couldn't figure it out.

PETER

The car was gone. He'd waited, hiding under the bed – the *bed*, for God's sake, as if that wouldn't have been the first place they'd look – for ten minutes after the car's engine started up. He felt stupid, standing at the window, pulling cobwebs and dustballs out of his hair, now that there weren't any dodgy-looking blokes peeking inside or lurking in the woods.

Everything looked so calm – a squirrel climbed up the side of a pine tree, a sparrow swooped to the ground and picked up a piece of dried twig. Could he have imagined the whole thing – had some kind of post-traumatic hallucination? Maybe it was a vision – a message from the spirit world, just as his mother's face had come to him so clearly, voicing such strange and unfamiliar words.

Maybe it was a warning.

Two figures appeared in the window – Jesus! Peter jumped back, heart catching, voice gasping. It was nobody dangerous, though – just Etta and that new boyfriend of hers. Hunkered down, more crouching than standing, they passed like fast-moving shadows, creeping toward the door.

So it must have been real. They must have seen the men, too. They must be scared – like him – must want to come back inside.

The door handle rattled in the kitchen. A fist pounded the glass.

'Peter?' The boy's voice.

Peter held his breath – waiting, thinking.

Seconds passed. A minute. The banging got louder.

'Come on, man. Give us a break.'

It was odd, this power. He could let them in, or he could keep them locked out. It was entirely up to him. He could force them to go back to that useless wigwam if he wanted, or he could let them into the cabin – *his* cabin – where there was a telephone, where there was food and water, where you could shutter the windows and lock the doors.

More pounding.

Idiots. Why wouldn't they stop? Why wouldn't they just piss off and leave him alone? People might hear them. Fishermen out on the lake, the neighbors the other side of the woods – what was their name? Nussbaum.

The fat guy with the gun. He'd hear the noise and come back. Is that what they wanted?

'Peter?' Etta was whining for him too. 'Could you let us in please?'

He hurried to the kitchen to open the door, not out of kindness or concern, he told himself, not because he was a decent bloke or a caring person. It wasn't that English sense of fair play, either.

No. He just needed to shut the wankers up.

As soon as the door was open, Etta pushed past him, shoved the Indian boy out of the way, and ran out of the kitchen, through the living room, off to the bedroom. Her face was red – had she been crying again?

Peter looked at Jonah, who seemed pretty messed up too – his face dirty, his hair all tangled. 'What the hell did you do out there?'

'What do you mean?' Jonah stood back, flinching, as if he thought Peter was about to hit him.

'You know what I mean,' Peter whispered through clenched teeth. He stepped forward again, his cheeks burning with jealousy and rage.

'No, I don't know.' Jonah had his hands out, playing the innocent.

Peter felt like spitting. 'Are you taking the piss or something?'

'The *what*?' Jonah pulled a face – still mocking him, still acting dumb.

'Do you want me to spell it out?'

The Indian boy shook his head.

Well, Peter *wouldn't* spell it out. Etta and Jonah. Alone. Laughing. He couldn't even bear to think about what else they might have been doing.

While Jonah glared at him, his lips curled in contempt, Peter backed away and stumbled through the kitchen doorway into the living room. He looked out the living room windows – *his* living room windows. Tall pine trees framed the view. The lake looked electric, glowing deep blue – the color of Etta's eyes – in the afternoon sun.

Jonah came into the room, stood beside him. 'All *right*,' he said. 'It was a stupid thing to do, I admit that. But I told her I was sorry, OK?'

'That's all you could do?' Peter sputtered. 'Apologize?'

'Look, I know what I did wasn't right, but I explained it to her – I tried to, at least – only she wouldn't listen.'

'And can you blame her?' The anger was welling

up inside him again. 'After all the things she's been through, for you to go and. . .'

He couldn't say it. He didn't even want to think it.

'OK,' Jonah sighed. He put his hands up, pretending to surrender, as he backed toward the door to the porch. 'OK. That's enough. You win.'

Jonah tapped the door open with his foot, letting the screen slam behind him. He jumped over the rotten, spongy steps, landing gracefully on the lawn. Peter thought about locking the door, refusing to let him come in again. It would serve him right, after what he'd done. Serve him right for spoiling things, for—

There was a noise in the bedroom – a gentle cough, Etta's footsteps, water running in the bath. Well, Etta was safe, at least. That was the main thing. The men, whoever they were, were gone.

Peter went to the door, looked out at the lake again. A family of ducks skimmed the shoreline, leaving tiny ripples in their wake. Jonah was at the edge of the woods, halfway down the hill. He was hunched over, back bent, digging his fingers into the soil at the base of a huge oak tree. He pulled something out of the earth, held it gently – a small plant, with a cluster of pink and white flowers. He put it to his lips, took a tiny bite before moving further towards the beach.

He made it look so natural, Peter thought – pick up a plant, smell it, eat it. That gnawing bitterness in his stomach twisted again. What had *he* been able to offer? A moldy sandwich. Two pieces of bruised English fruit.

Halfway down to the lake, Jonah stopped and looked out. Had he seen something, Peter wondered? Had the men come back? Jonah looked around restlessly, as though he weren't sure where he should go – back to the cabin, down to the lake, into the woods. He inched slowly up the hill, never taking his eyes off the water, never missing a backward step.

A second later, Peter heard what Jonah did – the sound of a boat, like the one from this morning, a clunky engine sputtering close to the shore. He moved towards the door and looked out onto the lake. The sound got louder, but Peter still couldn't see anything. Where was the bloody thing? Why wasn't it moving away?

Jonah stepped onto the porch and slipped silently through the door. 'Fishermen?' he whispered.

Peter's heart was still pounding and his throat was dry. He didn't dare answer, in case his voice cracked, so he just nodded, while he waited, holding his breath.

The engine sounds got smoother, the noise drifted away and, down on the beach, wavelets caused by the boat's wake lapped against the sand.

'And those other guys,' Jonah said, 'the ones with the shotgun – they were, like, hunters, right?'

Peter grunted something that sounded vaguely like 'yes'.

'They sure scared the hell out of Etta.' Jonah nodded toward the bedroom. 'She kinda flipped when that car pulled up – got all weird.'

'She must have thought they were the men she's running from.'

'What men?'

'Her mum's boyfriend and his gang – you know, the ones who shoved her into their car and. . .'

Jonah's face went red. Obviously, he didn't know about the men. That meant Etta hadn't told him. Suddenly, Peter felt a rush of pride, a swell of self-importance – the biggest loser on the football team had finally scored a goal.

'You *know* that's why she's here, don't you?' Peter didn't even try to get rid of the nasty, sneering tone in his voice.

'Woah,' Jonah said. 'She got, like, abducted? God, that's just—'

'Appalling? Disgusting?' He knew he sounded like some rent-a-Brit baddy in a cheap Hollywood film, but it was good – for once – to feel so superior.

'I said I was sorry, OK?' Jonah put his hands up – for real, this time. Then he turned around, went through the kitchen to the back door.

'I'm going out to the wigwam for a while,' he said, sighing. 'You should lock this place up, just in case those guys come back.'

'We'll be all right,' Peter said.

'No, seriously, you should—'

'I said we'll be all right.'

As Peter followed Jonah through the kitchen, something churned inside him again. What was it this time? Anger? 'You win,' Jonah had said. So why didn't he feel like a winner now, watching Jonah go outside and skulk back to the wigwam?

As he heard the door slam, he picked up the telephone receiver that had been left on the worktop. He listened for a dial tone to make sure it was still working, and carefully put it back in its proper place. Then he crept to the door and waited, counting one, two, three – all the way to ten – before turning the lock. He lifted the curtain and peeked out – at the empty driveway, the scrubby lawn, the scraggy line of trees at the edge of the forest.

He remembered what Etta had said that morning – trying to big him up while he sat on the sand and sobbed like a baby.

Thank you for saving me.

What if she'd seen him when the men came? It was almost funny, thinking back on it. The way he'd dived under the bed as soon as they got out of their car. The way he'd cowered in fear, trying desperately not to wet himself. And what would she think if she saw him now – hiding behind a locked door, twitching the curtains like a terrified old man?

Thank you for saving me.

Ha bloody ha.

Chapter Eleven

ETTA

The girl in the mirror – brushing her hair, working out the dried-stiff knots and tangles with her fingers – looked almost like me. Clean, clear-faced – no dirt or make-up streaks. She smelled nice, too, with that piny bath stuff still on her skin.

But she was wearing clothes she'd found in a stranger's closet. Frayed denim shorts that had to be held up with a safety pin and a Green Bay Packers tank top. And there was something different in her eyes – *my* eyes. They looked darker in the dim light – almost gray instead of blue. They seemed older, too, 'tired', like they say on TV, and I wanted to do what Mom did every time she passed a mirror – pull the skin back, make my face tighter and smoother, so I could go back to looking the way I did before.

I put down the brush. The clock by the side of the bed said 7:00, and it was getting dark outside, so I must have crashed out straight after taking the bath. 7:00. What would Mom be doing now? Sitting on the couch with Kyle. Putting on her uniform, if she got another waitress shift. Was she worried about me yet? Had she called the sheriff or the town cops? Maybe she had, maybe they'd be the next ones to come up the driveway. I could tell them everything then – about Kyle and the men and the guns and. . .

No. Kyle must have been telling the truth about her being in on it. Otherwise, a patrol car would have turned up by now. Isn't that what they did if somebody went missing – checked out all the barns and cabins and abandoned houses?

It was quiet outside. Bugs banged on the window, desperate to get through the screen to the bedside table lamp, bashing and crashing, like they just couldn't wait to get burned up. I listened for sounds from inside the cabin – Peter and Jonah were still here, weren't they? They hadn't bailed?

There was a clanging in the kitchen – somebody rattling pots and pans, running water in the sink. And there were voices, soft, at first – whispering – then getting louder, then somebody saying, '*Shoosh.*'

I went to the door, opened it a crack. I couldn't hear what they were saying, but I recognized Peter's accent, so the other guy must have been Jonah. I crept down into the living room. It was like a dungeon, eerie and silent. The curtains on the big windows were closed. The door to the porch was locked, a shade pulled down over the glass part. Only one light was on – a bright yellow rectangle spilled in from the kitchen doorway.

'Hey? You guys still here?'

'In here, Etta.' Peter's voice was hoarse, strained.

I stumbled through the dark room and felt my way to the kitchen. Jonah was at the sink, drying his hands on a kitchen towel. Peter was in front of the stove, watching a pan of water boil. Neither one of them looked up when I came in. It was like they were mad at me, like I'd done something wrong.

'I'll get those logs in,' Jonah said. He turned around and dropped the damp towel on the counter. 'See if they're dry enough for a fire.'

He still had his shirt off. When he saw me looking, he put his hands up over his bare chest and turned his back to me before sliding past. Peter acted embarrassed, too, even with all his clothes on. He fumbled with the pan on the stove, fiddled with the height of the flame. He dug around in a drawer and pulled out a big beat-up metal spoon. When it clattered onto the floor he let out a stream of swear words – the usual ones, plus a few English-sounding extras – as if dropping a kitchen utensil was the worst thing he'd ever done.

He was calmer by the time he picked up the spoon. It could have been the swearing – maybe he thought it made cooking more manly, like those British chefs on TV who are always having their words bleeped out.

'I told Jonah he could come in for some food,' Peter said, reaching into the cupboard above the stove, taking out the box of macaroni and cheese mix. He tore the top of the box with his fingers and poured the macaroni into the bubbling water.

'We were talking,' he said, 'Jonah and me.'

Uh-oh, I thought. That must have been what they were arguing about – me, about kicking me out, making me go back to Welmer because of the trouble I'd caused.

'Oh, yeah?' I tried to sound cocky, like I didn't give a damn what anybody said. If they wanted me to go, then fine, I'd just take off. No fussing, no whining, no begging to stay.

'Yeah, and, um. . .'

Why was he stammering? Why wouldn't he look at me?

'Well, we don't think those guys with the gun were looking for you.'

'Oh,' I said casually. So that was it. They weren't about to kick me out, but they didn't actually believe me, either.

'Jonah was saying they were just hunters – setting bait out for the autumn or something – and I think that must be right.' Peter jiggled the pan, lowered the flame. 'And that Charlie bloke. I mean, you didn't actually see him, did you?'

Peter turned around and looked at me. He had dark circles under his eyes like I did – the same hollow cheeks, too. 'What I'm thinking is that even if it *was* Charlie – even if he was your Charlie and he was looking for you, well he didn't find you, did he?'

I didn't say anything. I looked at the kitchen door. Locked tight. Good.

'So why would they come back?' Peter said. 'Those men with the gun. I mean, either way – what would be the point?'

We sat on the floor, eating Peter's macaroni and cheese in front of Jonah's fire.

Jonah was cross-legged, same as in the wigwam, but he seemed antsy, getting up every five minutes to poke the logs with a big metal stick. Once or twice he looked at me, his big eyes like dark pools, but he still didn't say anything about what had happened outside. No more explanations. No more excuses.

Peter leaned against the sofa that faced the big window. He didn't talk either. He gazed into the fire, lost in his own world. Jonah wanting to keep his mouth shut I could understand, but what was Peter's problem?

At least the fear had worn off a little. It had been six hours since the men had left, so what Peter said about them being hunters made sense. And even if it was Kyle's Charlie, he and the shovel kid *would* have come back by now if they thought we were here, wouldn't they?

Still, the silence – the not talking – made me nervous. There were too many strange noises from outside – crackles on the ground and swooshes in the wind and weird animal cries. Sounds from inside would be better, but there wasn't a TV, there wasn't a radio.

'I guess we'll have to tell each other stories,' I said, 'like in the olden days.'

'Don't know any,' Jonah muttered, his eyes fixed on the fire.

Peter coughed. Jonah looked at him sharply.

'Me neither,' Peter said. 'It'll have to be you.'

A story. I'd already told Peter about Kyle, and about Mom, and about all those other boyfriends of hers. There was the ghost of Grandma Hanson, but who wanted to hear about an old Norwegian lady who cleaned all the time? There was the story that Grandpa Vernon always told me about the night I was born. My dad was in it. A *real* story about my *real* dad – that was better than nothing, wasn't it?

'OK,' I said, 'but it's a Christmas story, so you have to imagine that it's cold outside, right? There's snow on the ground and there are icicles hanging down from the roof. And all the stores have Christmas decorations in the windows.'

Peter leaned back onto the sofa behind him, got comfortable. Jonah uncurled his legs. His eyes were closed – maybe that would help him listen. If it didn't, that was all right, too – I was only talking so I wouldn't have to hear.

'The real person who tells this story is my grandpa, because he was there when it happened. It was the night I was born and my mom went into labor. Nobody knew where my dad was so Grandpa had to go with Mom to the hospital and some babysitter was with my brothers in our apartment building.

'It didn't look much like Christmas at our place, Grandpa said. There was a crooked little artificial tree and a couple decorations but no lights, no tinsel, no angel on the top. There wasn't a single present under the tree, except the ones Grandpa brought.

'Anyway, I'm about to get born and Grandpa's at the hospital, signing all the papers and paying the bills – as usual – and he goes to the waiting room. And he waits, and he waits. And there are all these nervous fathers pacing the floor and Grandpa feels so bad that Mom hooked up with a loser like my dad. You know, like she deserved better and all that.'

Jonah opened his eyes. He picked up his stick, poked the fire.

'And then who turns up?' I asked.

'Your dad?' Jonah said, putting the stick down, interested now.

'Yep. High as a kite, Grandpa figured, and he had to go into the bathroom to do some kind of drug every five minutes, but he was there, that was the main thing. And he waited – same as the other dads. When I was born, the nurses let him hold me for a few minutes, and he cried. My own dad. He was so happy, Grandpa said. He broke right down and sobbed.'

'That's cool,' Jonah said.

Peter sat up straighter, shook his head like he was trying to keep awake.

'That's not the best part of the story, though. The really awesome part is when Grandpa goes back to the apartment to pick up my brothers at the neighbor's and tell them they had a baby sister. You'll never guess what he finds.'

I had to stop for a second, build up the suspense. This was my favorite part of the story. I didn't even have to close my eyes to see it. It was in front of me, like a picture on a TV screen, so real I could reach out and touch everything.

'There's a huge tree, way up to the ceiling, covered in colored lights that twinkle on and off, and there are piles of presents stuffed underneath. Not just cheap toys. I'm talking about expensive stuff – a Nintendo, a racing car set, a pink bassinet for me, and a stroller and clothes and dolls and rattles.

'Guess who did it?' I said. 'Guess who brought all that stuff over?'

Nobody answered. A burnt log dropped to the bottom of the fire. Peter glanced at Jonah, who picked up his stick and poked at the fire.

'Some elves?' Jonah said.

'No,' I laughed. 'My dad.'

'Oh,' Jonah said. Peter made a little 'hmmm' sound.

'My *real* dad,' I said, in case they didn't get it.

It was like a miracle, Grandpa always said, all those presents – like out of a movie.

'Well, that's it,' I said. 'That's my story.'

'Thanks,' Jonah mumbled, still staring at the fire.

'Yeah. Cheers, Etta.'

There was something weird in Peter's voice, like he couldn't wait for me to change the subject and talk about something else. My throat tightened and my face got hot. My stomach fluttered a little. I'd never told anyone that story before – that was one for Grandpa to tell me. That was my story, not theirs. *Our* story – mine and Grandpa's.

I should've kept my mouth shut.

It sounded stupid when I told them. My dad? Buying presents? Putting them under the tree like some crack-head Santa? What was the matter with me? That was probably what Peter and Jonah were thinking, too – how could Etta believe such a ridiculous lie?

Poor Grandpa. I couldn't blame him. My dad was a dead junkie and my mom was a good-for-nothing slut. No wonder he wanted to make me feel better about things. But, somehow, the lie – *his* lie – hurt more than the truth.

Outside, a bird thumped against the window. I gasped and jumped, started to get up so I could run and hide.

Peter touched my leg, rubbed his hand along my calf.

'It's nothing,' he whispered. 'It's OK.'

I wanted to laugh. Nothing? OK?

I pushed his hand away. He could say whatever he wanted about hunters or trappers – I knew the truth. This time it was a bird banging at the window, next time it would be the barrel of a gun. I might as well hit the road right now, make my way back to Welmer, walk into the trailer acting all apologetic, tell Mom *another* bunch of lies about how I'd run away and how it was all my fault.

I looked into the fire and pictured it: me and Mom – like in the old days, before we had to move all the time. I saw a beige tiled kitchen in some tiny apartment. She was cooking spaghetti sauce, splattering grease and tomato juice all over the wall, and we were singing along to the radio.

That was another memory that probably never even happened. But it made me think about how alike we were, me and Mom. The way we both talked like smart-asses but then did exactly what people told us to do. 'Get in the car.' I got in the car. 'Stay in the wigwam.' I stayed put. 'Believe a bunch of stupid crap.' I swallowed every word.

By now the fire was just a single wave of flickering light and most of the firewood had turned to ashes. Jonah sat up again, gave the last glowing log one more push.

No. I wouldn't go home. Not now. Not ever. I wouldn't fall for any more lies, either, or listen to stupid fairy tales about things turning out for the best. I wasn't going to pay any attention to what other people said. From now on I'd do what *I* wanted to do. And if people did bad things to me, well, I'd do bad things right back.

PETER

He shouldn't have touched her. The way she had slapped his hand off – could she have made her revulsion any more obvious?

He should've listened to her story, too. He caught bits of what she said – drugs, birth, something about icicles – but his mind was still plagued by a different story. He couldn't stop thinking about what Etta and Jonah had been doing out in the wigwam. They'd been out there for how long – an hour? They'd had time to get up to all sorts. Kissing. Touching. More if they'd wanted to, and they probably did.

Worse than all that, he kept imagining Jonah's bravery as the gun guy's car pulled in. No cowering behind curtains or hiding under a bed like a poncey Englishman. No, Jonah would've used his body as a shield, offered to give up his own life to protect Etta's honour, manfully wielding his decorated club.

It hurt Peter even to look at Jonah now. It wasn't fair – the looks, the muscles. He was tall, dark and

216

handsome, like a bronze statue in the glow of the fire. How could Peter's pale skin and nondescript features ever compete with that? And with Jonah's bravery thrown into the mix, Peter didn't stand a chance.

It was stupid – he knew that – worrying about what he looked like, when twice in the past twenty-four hours he had thought he was going to be killed. Maybe the nasty jolt of seeing the gun guy was starting to wear off, along with the other shocks he'd had since he left England – Etta tumbling out of the car in the darkness, their flight through the woods, the discovery of Jonah squatting on his mother's land in a ramshackle shed.

Had that only been yesterday? Only this morning? It didn't make sense.

Funny how it wasn't *those* things that were playing on his mind, but the fact that some other bloke had stolen his girl. And that was the funniest of the lot – until that moment, he hadn't realized that he thought of Etta that way, as *his* girl. Up to now, they had been friends, companions in a crisis, nothing more.

But she seemed different tonight. Sitting against the firelight, he noticed things. Her eyes were dark and intense as she told her story. Her hair was lovely too, since she'd had a bath – soft and feathery, so light and smooth that he wanted to touch it. Her clean clothes were just cast-offs from one of the cupboards – cropped denims, a faded American football vest, but he could see the small, gentle curves under the thin, loose top. So when she got up in panic after the bird hit the glass he'd wanted to put his arms around her, not just lamely brush her leg, and not just to calm her down or soothe her fears. He wanted to hold her, to kiss her, to. . .

Peter shook his head. This was stupid. No, worse than that, it was *wrong* – Etta trusted him, Etta was his friend, and here he was thinking about her like some. . .

He closed his eyes so he couldn't see her any more. That was all he could do for the moment – turn away, squeeze his eyes as tightly as he could, try not to think of her, try to erase all the beautiful images that popped into his head.

JONAH

Jonah inched toward the dying fire. The embers were still hot and his bare chest felt as though it was getting burned – a good feeling. He moved closer still. The pain became more intense. Even better.

He stayed still, changed his breathing when the pain got unbearable, remembering, weirdly, his mother's birth story that she thought was so funny – the nurses telling her to breathe through the pain, her swearing at them and demanding drugs, them refusing to give her any, her having to pant frantically like a demented chimp.

He tried it, silently – short, sharp bursts of air through rounded lips. No relief. Even the satisfying sensation of self-punishment was disappearing. It just hurt, making his eyes well up with tears, making his body flinch and twist away from the fire.

He gave up, scuttling away from the tormenting heat. It wouldn't be enough, anyway, not enough to burn away the shame he felt about what he'd done.

'You want me to put another log on?'

Peter grunted sleepily. Etta shrugged.

Was it deliberate, this cold shoulder treatment? Hadn't he grovelled enough out in the wigwam? He'd said sorry, hadn't he – to both of them. He was trying to make it up to them now, couldn't they see that? What more could he do?

'I'll go out to the porch and get one.'

Another grunt. Another shrug.

To hell with them, Jonah thought. He stepped over Etta's legs. He sidled past the chair that Peter pretended to be sleeping against so he wouldn't have to look at him.

The back porch creaked as he stepped onto it, seeming to list even further away from the cabin, down the hill and toward the lake, which was just visible through the scraggly fringe of pine trees that grew along the path to the water's edge. Jonah longed to be there again, alone, cross-legged on the sand, around an open fire, looking up at the multitude of bright stars, no company other than the sound of fish jumping on the lake, leaping for joy at the pale light of the silvery moon. He was tired of being cooped up in the cabin, the white man's cabin, just because he was afraid of a couple of hunters.

Dutifully, he reached into the rotting barrel containing the logs. He took one out, shook off the cobwebs, brushed away the bugs, carried it back inside.

Again, he got no thanks. Again, he got nothing but a glance and nod from Etta.

'Look, I'm getting sick of being locked up here like a prisoner. I'm going down to the lake. Anybody want to come along?'

Neither of them seemed to hear him. Etta eventually shook her head. Peter didn't move.

'Whatever.'

He dumped the log onto the fire, causing the embers to leap back into life and lick the log with hungry tongues. He jabbed it with the poker, centering it snugly. This would burn until they were asleep.

'I'll probably sleep in the wigwam tonight. I doubt if those hunting guys'll be back.'

Why wouldn't one of them just talk to him? His mother would do this sometimes, sit in the living room with no lights on, for hours sometimes, smoking cigarette after cigarette, swilling red wine in an oversized glass, watching the ruby liquid glow in the dim light that shone through from outside. There was nothing he could do to pull her out of it, no words of apology or comfort that would make her open up again, let him near her again.

He waited at the doorway for one of them to open their mouths.

'OK then. If that's how it is.'

He let the screen door slam on his way out.

The lake was calling him, gently, like his only friend. The insects droned a chant of welcome.

PETER

Peter felt a twinge of triumph. Etta hadn't begged Jonah to stay. She hadn't thrown herself at him or volunteered to join him outside.

He was still able to play his ace. All right, so he wasn't handsome or strong or brave, like Jonah, but he had something to offer that the alpha male Indian couldn't match – solid walls, a cabin with proper locks on the doors.

'Do you think he'll be all right out there?' Etta asked. She looked at Peter, her eyes wide with concern. God, she was so lovely in this light.

'Of course.'

'You really think those guys are just hunters?'

'Probably.'

Etta looked anxiously at the back door as if she wanted to go out onto the porch and call Jonah back. He should have said, 'Definitely.' That would have sounded manlier, more authoritative.

'Listen, if Kyle had really wanted to find you,

wouldn't he have come himself?'

Etta nodded. 'I guess so.' She relaxed a bit, sat back against the chair that Jonah had just been crouching in front of.

'We'll be OK,' Peter said.

'Please don't say that,' she whispered. 'No more lies.'

She looked like she was going to cry again. If only he dared move closer to her, put his arm around her reassuringly. 'I mean it,' he said. 'Mum used to say nothing bad could ever happen at Yellow Lake.'

Etta breathed in deeply, let out a half-sung sigh.

'Tell me about your mom. Your mum, I mean.'

Peter edged back, leaned away from the glowing embers that now seemed dangerously hot. Once again, his eyes stung with tears. He remembered that morning – *this* morning – on the beach. The wracking sobs, the uncontrollable crying – he couldn't give her a repeat performance now. He wanted to show Etta strength, not weakness – bravery, not grief.

'What did she die of?'

He swallowed. Just say it. 'Cancer.'

Hopefully that would be enough for her.

'What kind of cancer?'

'The kind that kills you.'

'Oh.'

He could tell from her voice that he'd hurt her. What the hell was the matter with him? All she did was ask an innocent question. All she did was offer a bit of kindness, so why did he have to sound so nasty? Why did he snap back at her like a vicious dog?

'Sorry,' he said. 'I don't know what gets into me sometimes.'

She looked so small beside the huge open fire, so vulnerable. He wouldn't blame her if she moved away from him, or if she slipped outside to spend the night with Jonah.

She sighed again, edging back towards him. Maybe he was just imagining this. He could hardly believe it, after the way he'd spoken. But it seemed that she wanted him to touch her, that she wanted him to put his arms around her.

So that's what he did. He wrapped his arms around her slender shoulders as if he were a huge bird with enormous wings that could shield her, warm her, protect her. As she fell into his body like a limp doll, her head collapsed onto his chest, and she cried.

'I'm sorry too,' she said.

'Don't be,' Peter whispered. 'It's just . . . it happened so fast, she died before I had the chance. . .'

Etta didn't say any more, and Peter realized that

it probably wasn't Mum she was talking about. But what did she have to be sorry for? What had Etta ever done wrong?

Whatever it was, it didn't matter any more. Whatever either of them had said or done in the past wasn't important. They were together, safe. Peter and Etta at Yellow Lake. That's what counted – nothing else.

He smoothed her hair until she settled, like he had the night before in the woods, as a comfort, another layer of protection. She was so close to him now. His mouth was nearly touching her soft, plump lips but he didn't dare kiss her. It was as if the darkness had paralysed him, or as if Etta had cast a magical spell that made time stand still and movement impossible.

The moment was melted away by the fire's warmth, but they stayed like that – together, but still apart – until Peter felt something moist soak through his thin T-shirt onto his skin. Peter looked down, gently lifted Etta's head.

She wasn't crying any more. She was asleep, and snoring. Her pretty mouth was open, and she was drooling on him.

Chapter Twelve
— ETTA

Morning was shining through the window. I sat up and looked out. Sunshine sparkled on Yellow Lake like millions of diamonds. The sky was pale blue, cloudless.

Like Peter's eyes.

Even before I opened my eyes, I sensed him across the room, moving, breathing. He was asleep in the small bed in the corner, snoring gently. The covers were pulled over his head, so just a tuft of spiky white hair stuck out, like the tassel on a stalk of corn.

He must have stayed in the room with me so I'd feel safer. After last night, we were back to being Hansel and Gretel again. Brother and sister. Friends. At least that's how it seemed in the perfect light that was bringing me peace and calm.

Or was it more than that now? Were *we* more than that? I couldn't tell. Something had happened last night, but I wasn't sure what it was. I tried to piece things together. Jonah had left to go down to the lake. Peter and I had talked. He had told me something about his mother. I had cried. He had dried my tears, held me.

And after that? What had happened?

Remember, I thought. Remember.

It came to me then. His arms, the way they trembled, like he was scared of hurting me. His face. The sweet smell of his warm breath against my cheek. Had he kissed me then?

I pulled the blanket around me, closed my eyes and listened to the sounds of the trees – that gentle brushing noise, like a dry tinkling. Under the windows something scuffled. A harmless creature – a tiny mouse or a soft squirrel – was rooting for food.

I looked out onto the lake – a shimmering sheet of gold and silver – and I knew that everything was different, better.

We would start again – me, Peter.

Jonah, too, if he wanted.

JONAH

Jonah was on the beach, curled up, shivering in the damp coolness of early morning. Something nudged his senses out of sleep – the smell of oil and metal, the sound of a motor churning up water along the shoreline, whirring and buzzing like an angry wasp.

'Hey, you.'

Completely awake now, Jonah kept his eyes closed, faking sleep while he tried desperately to recognize the voice, place it somewhere in his memory.

'Hey! Whatcha doing?'

Slowly, he opened his eyes to a narrow slit, allowing in a hazy image of harsh silhouettes against the low sun. Two men were in a bobbing boat, the engine still running, ten feet from where he was huddled. It was too late to run and hide in the woods. No, he'd have to sit up and speak to these men – one of them slim, sitting, the other one fat, standing with stumpy legs wide apart for balance, fishing rod in his hand, held like a weapon.

'This here's private property, you know, so you better get moving.'

The skinny one, whose hand was on the motor, revved it a couple of times for effect. The fat man made waving motions with his fishing rod that left circular traces on the lids of Jonah's squinting eyes.

Slowly, Jonah sat up, the words 'no sudden moves' lodging themselves into his head, as if this were a movie, the men were armed cops, and he was about to be cuffed and restrained. He smiled and gave a little wave.

'Morning, guys. How's it going out there today?'

The fat man looked at him suspiciously. He eyed the fat man, too – was this the guy with the gun? It could've been, but this man had sunglasses and a baseball cap on and besides, all fat white guys looked pretty much the same. The skinny kid wasn't the weasel boy, though. This kid was younger, twitchier, red-faced, more of a chipmunk.

'You from the Cities?'

The boy clicked the engine into gear, as if he were cocking a gun. Obviously a brown-skinned, long-haired kid from Minneapolis posed a real threat.

'Up by Anoka,' Jonah lied.

The gear went into neutral again. Anoka, where was that, the man seemed to be wondering. Anoka – nice name for a town. He'd heard of it, anyway, and he couldn't remember reading about any gang type of stuff there. Anoka. Yeah, that'd be safe enough.

'Well, you know, this ain't Anoka, boy. People ain't always friendly around here. They ain't used to strangers, so I'd be careful if I was you.'

Jonah laughed. The guy was joking, right? 'I think I'll be OK.'

But the man didn't smile back. He shifted his stance, crouching slightly as if, despite his fat belly, he could pounce like a cat. 'You get your Indian ass back to Anoka before I call the sheriff, and you'll be just fine.'

Chipmunk boy revved the engine again, a cue for the man to sit down so they could get back home and make that call. 'Come on, Charlie. We got things to do.'

Charlie. Jesus. The name boomed through Jonah's head like a cannon shot. How many fat guys named Charlie lived around here?

'I mean it, Injun. Sign says no trespassing. Can't you read?'

Before Jonah could say anything, before he could

take a better look at the fat guy just to make *sure*, the chipmunk had turned the boat around, and was steering it away from the shore, out onto the lake, into the path of the sun's punishing rays.

ETTA

We turned the three eggs and the last of the Velveeta into an omelette and shared it out equally, with a garnish of shrivelled-up apple chunks that Peter had taken off the plane from England. We ate in the kitchen, leaning against the countertops. The food tasted like a salty, dried-up sponge. I wanted to spit it out in the garbage can, but I knew the cupboards were empty, so I choked down every disgusting mouthful.

It was still a beautiful morning. Through the living room window the rising sun was making that sparkly dance on the water, but the feelings I'd woken up with – the peace, the calm – were gone.

Charlie had come back. Next it'd be Kyle.

Jonah was still shaking from what had happened down on the beach. 'I thought he was going to pull out a gun and shoot me, man.'

Peter carried on like nothing had happened. He finished his food, rinsed off our plates and set them carefully in the sink. He strolled over to the kitchen door and opened it wide. He stepped outside, looked around. What was he doing – trying to prove to Jonah and me that *he* wasn't scared?

'Who says it's even the same person?'

'I say, and I'm the one who saw him,' Jonah said. 'He was fat, his face was red.'

Peter came back into the kitchen without locking the door. 'That could be any one of a hundred blokes around here.'

'Well, this dude was named Charlie, same as the gun guy,' Jonah said. 'C'mon, Peter, what more do you want?'

Peter took a dish-towel out of a drawer and dried the plates he'd rinsed. He opened another cupboard and put them on a shelf.

'It was Charlie,' I said. '*Kyle's* Charlie. Come on, Peter, you know it as well as I do.'

He glanced at me, his face stony, blank. 'No, I don't.'

Jonah pushed past him and dumped his plate into the sink, clattering the silverware onto the metal draining board. He went to the front door and closed it tightly, turning the lock. He looked out the tiny curtained window. His shoulders were heaving up and down. Was he crying? Too angry to talk?

Finally, he turned around.

'I'm making this shit up, Peter – is that what you think?'

Peter didn't answer. His jaw was tight, like he'd turned into stone.

Jonah came back into the kitchen.

'Why would I do that?' he said, standing close to Peter, squaring up.

Peter answered quickly, as if the answer had been with him for days, and he'd been waiting for the right time to say it. 'So you could come back inside. So you can stay here with us.'

'What?'

Jonah's eyes widened like a little kid's. He backed away from Peter, his face soft, his lips trembling.

'You know that's bullshit,' he stammered.

'Do I?'

'Why would I want to stay here with you, when I've got my own place outside?'

'Come on, Jonah.' Peter's face had changed, too. It got red, like he was embarrassed or angry or ashamed. He looked at me, then back at Jonah. 'Don't make me say it.'

What was Peter talking about? Was he accusing Jonah of being a coward? Did he know about what had happened out in the wigwam? Was he rubbing it in?

Then it was Jonah's turn – he looked at Peter, then me. I felt like the pointless female in a movie, only in the scene so the men could fight over her.

Peter took a big breath, and let the words tumble out. 'You were happy enough outside until *she* came along.'

She.

Boom. There it was.

She. Not a person, not *Etta*, just a *she*. One notch up from an *it*.

'I'm still here,' I said. I had to force the words out, over the balled-up knot of anger and hurt that thickened my tongue.

This was Peter talking. *My* Peter.

'So please don't talk like—'

The phone rang – a harsh, high-pitched jangle, stopping me in mid-sentence, shutting me up.

It rang again – twice, three times.

Kyle.

'Don't answer it,' Jonah said.

Peter sighed, put his hand on the receiver. He looked at Jonah and raised his eyebrows, like a sicko holding a loaded gun.

'Please,' Jonah pleaded. 'It'll be *them*.'

Peter shrugged. 'So what' – that's what his body said.

He looked at Jonah, tapping his fingers on the side of the phone while it rang and rang – five times, six.

'For God's sake,' Jonah said. 'Leave it.'

The dried food churned in my stomach suddenly, like a heavy weight that was trying to lift itself out. I stumbled out of the kitchen, went through the living room, the bedroom – there was my unmade bed – and into the bathroom. I stood over the toilet, gagging and sputtering. My teeth chattered, my eyes watered and something burned in the back of my throat. My stomach heaved but no food came out – just a line of thin, sour-tasting drool.

In the kitchen, the rings seemed to be getting louder. It was like an alarm was sounding, with each sharp clang scraping away the fog in my head, sending out the warning, 'You're on your own here, girl. Jonah will leave you again if you give him the chance. Peter doesn't care any more, if he ever did at all.'

PETER

Peter picked up on the tenth ring, while Jonah stood in the doorway.

'Hello?'

Peter waited, dreading his father's clipped, icy tones.

'Say, gee, is that . . . is Ken there? Ken Robinson?'

Who was this? Not his dad. Not Uncle Kenneth. And from the confused drawl, not some gun-toting low life either.

'I'm sorry, but my uncle's not here at the moment.' Peter laid on the accent, poshing up the vowels, clipping the cononsants. 'This is his nephew. From England. May I be of help?'

'Oh, no. I'm from the sheriff's office. Deputy Ed Johnson. Just doing some checking.'

'What seems to be the problem, Deputy Johnson?'

In the doorway, Jonah's eyes widened.

'We got a call from somebody who saw some suspicious types walking around by your uncle's cabin. You ain't seen anybody who fits that description?'

'No, sir.' Peter was proud of himself – he remembered that Americans liked to be called 'sir'.

'Well.' The man at the other end had run out of words. He'd been doing his duty, that was all. To him the phone call was something to tick off on his to-do list. It was nothing worth getting worked up about.

'OK then. It was pro'ly you they saw, but if you notice anything funny-looking, give us a shout.'

Peter hung up. In spite of his bravado, his hands were shaking. He hoped Jonah hadn't noticed. He was glad Etta couldn't see.

Etta. He'd have to grovel an apology, make things right again.

Meanwhile, Jonah's dark eyes were still flashing anger and fear.

'It was nothing,' Peter said casually. 'Somebody from the sheriff's office, asking if we'd seen ourselves.'

He shoved past Jonah, barely resisting the temptation to give him a sharp dig in the ribs with his elbow. He went into the alcove bedroom, wishing that there was a door for him to slam or kick, not just a curtain to rustle.

Why was Jonah still here, anyway, he wondered as he hurled himself onto the bed. Why didn't he just piss off back to Minneapolis or Chicago or wherever he was from? If he was too much of a wuss to stay in that hut that he'd built with his bare hands, that 'wigwam' that supposedly meant so much to him, then why didn't he just give up and go home?

That sounded like a good idea.

Give up and go home.

This had all been a big mistake, he could see that now, coming here in the first place, then dragging Etta along. She would've been better off if he'd just left her there on the side of the road.

He turned over on the bed and faced the pine ceiling. How many times had he stared at this when he was little, thinking the knots were part of some elaborate treasure map when they were nothing but resin flaws in discolored wood? And this bedroom wasn't the secret cave of his childhood imagination. It was more like a tomb – claustrophobic and stuffy.

The truth was, he didn't belong here. This was no more his spiritual home than it was Jonah's or even Etta's. It was just an old, broken-down shack that his uncle would do well to offload onto somebody who'd tear it down and build something nicer, more solid, with proper foundations. And the three of them – Jonah, Etta, himself – they were nothing more than a trio of self-pitying whingers.

So Etta's mother was a selfish, neglectful slag and her stepfather was dodgy? Not exactly a groundbreaking case. And poor Jonah felt torn between two cultures? Join the bleeding line. Everybody's mixed up in some way. Nobody cares.

And his own problem? Mother. Cancer. Dead.

Not fair.

Oh really? Think you're the only kid this has happened to?

Not fair.

Tell me something I haven't heard before, sunshine.

Not. Fucking. Fair.

Oooh, now we're getting somewhere, mate.

Not fucking fair, I said.

Peter curled himself into a tiny, hedgehogged ball. He clutched the nubby bedspread, twisted the tiny bumps between his thumbs and forefingers. His stomach burned as though he'd been stabbed by a rusty knife. The pain spread through his body like a slow, black, bleed.

God, he missed her. *She* was the one he needed, not

his father, not these new so-called friends – not even Etta.

Mum. *She* was the only one who had ever loved him and now she was gone.

Self-pity rolled over him. It crashed against him like a wave, keeping him nailed to the bed, his arms wrapped round his head as if for protection, a relentless rush of grief and anger, of hatred for every person who wasn't his mother, who was still alive, who was still left in his life like a useless appendage – his father, his mates in England and, most of all, Etta and Jonah for bringing him nothing but trouble and a brand new form of misery and heartache.

He lay there as though he were in a coma, a coma in which he was unable to move, but could still sob like a baby. How long was he like that – a minute? An hour? Gradually, he felt something else wash over him – smooth water, warm and calm. He could breathe properly, slow and easy. He could turn over onto his back, stretch out his body.

Then, finally, he slept.

ETTA

I was almost ready to go.

I'd taken an old backpack that was hanging on a hook in the bedroom closet. It had tiny holes in the bottom from where a mouse had been chewing but it was sturdy enough to hold what I was taking – my old, dirty clothes, another clean T-shirt from the chest of drawers, a washcloth, a pillowcase, a green stripy towel, a thin polyester blanket.

I went into the bathroom. I opened the door of the medicine cabinet, trying not to look at my face in the mirror. I took out the things I needed – a sliver of soap, a half-empty tube of toothpaste, an old toothbrush with flattened bristles. Nobody would miss them, would they? There were shampoo miniatures on the side of the bathtub, too. I picked up one that was from a Las Vegas casino. I picked up another one from the North Pines Lodge, where Mom worked. We had a whole cupboard full of those tiny bottles back at the trailer – shampoo, conditioner, body lotion. I held the bottle, tempted to take a big sniff and remind myself of home.

No. There wasn't time now. I'd do it later, once I was on the road, maybe at some gas station, washing in a sink.

I slipped the pack over my shoulders, adjusted the straps until it fit just right. There. All ready. All set to hit the open road.

I went back into the bedroom and looked out the windows, first onto the front lawn – the driveway, the woods, the road. I listened for traffic but there was nothing out there. Nobody. Just me and the breeze sifting through the trees. I crossed the room and looked out at the lake. The high sun bleached out the color so it was a light blue gray. The water was glassy, calm.

I needed to go outside one more time. It would only take a few minutes. Just long enough to take a picture in my head of the tiny waves on the beach, the tufty grass growing up out of the sand, the sound of birds singing in the tree-tops and squirrels jumping from branch to branch.

I crept out of the bedroom, feeling like a thief with my stolen bag full of used toiletries. I unlocked the door and stepped onto the porch, not daring to turn around in case Peter was watching.

I went halfway down the hill and sat down. Jonah was on the beach, standing over a pile of wood. His body was covered in sweat and dirt as he walked in a circle around the wood, his arms held high. There were bits of color – his decorated club was sticking out from the top of the woodpile, one of the pictures from the wigwam dangled from a piece of bark.

He bent over and in a few minutes smoke rose up.

What was he burning? I saw a big square of birch, some pointed sticks.

It was the wigwam! What had he done – torn it down? Dragged it to the beach?

For a second I wanted to run to the bottom of the hill and put out the fire. What was Jonah doing, destroying something he'd built with his own hands, burning something he loved so much?

But as the flames leapt higher, I understood. Better him than somebody else.

Better to hurt yourself than be hurt by others.

The smoke rose up the hill like a cloud of incense. It smelled sweet – he must have been burning something else, too, the plants and herbs I'd seen, drying on the floor. The scent reminded me of fall and the things I'd normally be doing by now – getting ready for school, making last-minute shopping trips with my friends, going down to stay with Grandpa and the Duchess for a few days.

But I wouldn't be doing any of those things, not this fall, probably not ever again.

I couldn't go home, so none of the other things would happen either. Seeing Grandpa was out of the question and so was going to school. And my friends? They were a long way from Welmer, and even further from here.

So where did that leave me? On my own, with no one to worry about me or care what I did.

Maybe that wasn't such a bad thing. I could go north, hitch a ride to Duluth, get on a Lake Superior ferry or one of those big ships, hide in the back of somebody's car or truck and sneak into Canada. Nobody'd ever think to look for me there.

Jonah threw on another piece of wood. The fire spat and crackled as the flame leapt higher. All the while he was saying something, words I couldn't make out, humming them in a deep, droning voice. Then he crouched down facing the lake, away from the cabin, away from me. All I could see was his bare back and the bony ribcage that poked through his skin like giant fingers. He looked starving – it was time for him to go home.

He was scared, too. Even from here, he looked twitchy. He kept looking up and out to the lake, twisting his head round, like he was hearing voices or feeling some mysterious presence. I knew what I was scared of – Kyle and those gun guys – but what was Jonah's problem? Was it what he'd done in the wigwam, the way he'd run and left me alone? Maybe he *had* seen those horror movies after all, and knew the fate that was coming to him – being chopped up by an axe-murderer and fed to the wolves, falling into a pit full of brain-sucking zombies, getting his leg caught in a bear trap and slowly bleeding to death.

He stood up, turned his head to the sky, raised his arms. He put his hands into the smoke, then touched his body all over, like he was washing himself. The smoke got darker, stronger. It blew up the hill straight into my eyes, making them tear up. The smell was like a weird perfume. It made me feel dizzy, but in a good way, like being a little drunk. The lake seemed to dance in front of my eyes, the trees looked bendy. The smoke made me want to smile, to laugh.

The smell made me want to stay at Yellow Lake forever.

PETER

The smoke wafted up from Jonah's fire on the beach, and infused Peter's dreams, intensifying the pictures in his mind. His mother's spirit was with him – although he couldn't see her any more – lying on the bed, holding him, rubbing his hair, keeping him safe. And he didn't mind. He didn't duck her hugs, or flinch away from her touch as he had when she was still alive. He didn't close his eyes in terror the way he had when she was dying. He let himself melt into her comforting arms, like a baby.

She was murmuring voiceless words – shapeless sounds – that he couldn't make out. They were peaceful and soothing, nothing like the noises he remembered her making when she was alive.

'Listen,' she said. 'Listen.'

He heard music, something played on a wooden flute, high-pitched but mellow. The music came from his tiny bedroom, from the cabin itself, from which it permeated the air like a slow mist or a dense, warm cloud.

Things got blurry, distorted, as if this sound was covering his face. Still he could hear her voice.

'Listen, listen.'

Still he could feel her presence, and the beat of her heart like distant thunder.

'Listen, listen.'

The cabin music got quieter as other sounds intruded on his sleep – crunching, slamming, shuffling. His mother's voice persisted, even as the sounds of the outside world grew louder, but the words became less audible. They were words, though, they brought meaning.

'Don't be afraid.'

Those were the words he sensed as her soothing grip on his body gently let go. 'Don't be afraid.' He struggled against wakefulness. He wanted to stay where he was, with Mum, but he felt something forcing him back into reality, a tugging, as if he was being trussed and hoisted upwards, lifted into the sky by a piece of gossamer cabling.

The sounds that woke him were cars.

'Listen.'

More than one this time – that was obvious from the

crunching on the driveway, the slamming of doors, the chorus of low male voices.

Peter pounced silently off the bed. He crept into the kitchen. The door was locked. The window's thin curtain was slightly open. . .

The gun guys were back.

There were two cars, and four men were outside them, huddling together, nodding, glancing into the cars, then towards the woods.

There was another thing, too, but before he could make sense of what he was seeing, something pulled at him, dragging him away from the door, hauling him back into the living room, pointing him towards the windows.

The others. Etta and Jonah. He'd forgotten about them.

He opened the door, careful not to make any sound, and stepped onto the porch. Jonah couldn't possibly have heard him from the beach, but he stepped away from his fire, turned toward the cabin and bounded up the hill in huge, effortless strides. Etta moved instantly, too – caught up in Jonah's swift-footed wake.

It was as if an invisible rope had bound them together. All Peter had to do was tug at it, and it hoisted them safely and silently back inside.

Moments later, as Etta crumpled into his arms, and Jonah locked the door behind him, Peter realized the other thing he'd seen through the window.

Inside the cars were four more men, two in each back seat. They were sitting completely still, like mannequins or dummies. Bound and gagged, Peter thought

Maybe already dead.

JONAH

His fire had burned in vain. The spirits hadn't answered his prayers. Bravery was what he'd asked for, a way to make amends, to heal the shame of his cowardice. All he felt was fear.

Still, as Peter and Etta stumbled towards the bedroom, he managed to pull shut the living room curtains. None of the men he'd seen had been around this side of the cabin before, so they wouldn't have known whether they were opened or closed. Less exposed, comforted by the darkened room, he moved back into the kitchen. There was no one standing outside the window over the sink. No one was peering in through the small sheer curtain on the door, either, so it was safe to look out. He bent down to a crouch and slowly edged to the door. He straightened up.

Out on the driveway, the men were still standing by their cars in a close huddle, heads locked together, nodding, agreeing on something.

Jonah recognized Charlie straight away – how could he ever have doubted that it was the same person? The weasel boy with the shovel was there, too. So was the younger one who drove the boat and looked like a chipmunk.

There was another man, a biker type with a beard and wiry, blonde hair, who acted as if he were in charge. He nodded at the tied-up men inside the car, then pointed to a spot in the woods. He took out a pack of cigarettes and the other three scrambled to get a light for him. While they fumbled in their pockets, he looked towards the cabin, cocking his head, holding his hand up to shade his eyes from the sun.

Jonah ducked into a crouch.

He knows we're in here.

He slouched towards the living room, his heart thumping shamefully, his hands shaking like a cowardly child's.

Then he remembered – he still had some herbs left. He took them out of his pocket and walked into the living room, scattering the dry crushed leaves onto the wooden floor, grinding them with his bare heel into the woven braid rug in front of the fireplace, until all that was left on his hands was a powdery dust. He covered his face and breathed in the sweet aroma. He closed his eyes and sang under his breath the line of an Ojibwe prayer he'd learned from the internet – the only line he remembered.

That was all he could do for now – pray, chant.

The rest was up to the spirits.

The blonde boy and the girl – why couldn't he remember their names? – came out of the bedroom. The girl took hold of his arm, led him away with her, saying frightened words in a language he couldn't make any sense of – it was English, right? It had to be, so why couldn't he understand her?

Then everything around him went quiet – as though he'd smashed into a wall of silence.

Whoa, he thought. What's going on?

He followed the girl into another room, helpless, stumbling, falling into a hole where the world disappeared and visions came – people were dancing around a fire, lighting up the darkness.

This is cool he thought. Weird, but cool.

Sounds filled his head – drums, chanting and singing. A prayer – his prayer.

He smiled and closed his eyes, humming along with the music, mumbling the words. He wasn't afraid any more because he knew what was happening. This was all for him, and for his friends – Etta, Peter, that's what they were called. The spirits were with them, keeping them safe.

PETER

Get to the phone. Call 999. No. 911. Which one was it?

Peter hunkered down, half-crawling back into the kitchen. He checked the door again – locked, but what difference did it make? If the men wanted to get in, they could have it down in minutes. No – seconds. Maybe he could shore it up in some way. There would be tools, hardware somewhere. He tried a drawer – a hammer, a chisel, some nails, a box of screws. Then he crawled into the store cupboard. There was a stepladder hanging on the wall, there were a few pieces of timber. . .

He scuttled back to the kitchen. What the hell was he thinking? The men outside would hear the pounding. They'd rush the door, break it down in an instant, shoot him dead right there in the kitchen.

Just call. *911*. That was it.

He reached up for the phone. Stretching the cord into the hallway so that he could still see out the window, he dialled and counted the rings. One, two, three. An answer. A confident female voice. He asked for the sheriff's department, and she put him straight through.

'Sheriff's office. Bryson.'

A man's calm, deep voice. *Bryson.* Was that the name of nice guy who'd called earlier to find out if they were OK? He had that same small-town lilt that made every man sound like Uncle Ken.

'Yes. Yes, I'd like to report some men. They're in cars. And they're trespassing on private property, and they have guns.'

'OK.' The deputy on the phone spoke slowly, dragging out each syllable, as if there were nothing to worry about. Even words like 'trespassing' and 'guns' didn't seem to be setting off any alarms. Was carrying a gun completely normal around here?

'Are they behaving in a threatening manner?'

Peter's voice was a harsh whisper. 'Threatening?' He was gasping for air, trying not to break down and cry. 'They've got men tied up.'

Silence.

'And guns. Did I say about the guns?'

Nothing. Didn't the man *care*?

'Hurry, please,' Peter croaked. 'They're going to do something dreadful.'

'I *heard* you,' the man said.

Another silence was followed by a rustling sound like the shifting of papers, then a squeak, like the man on the phone was one of those fat TV cops, twirling around in a swivelling chair.

'And where is the property located?' The man's voice had changed. It was still the same person, but he didn't talk like a nice uncle any more. He sounded mechanical and unnatural, as if his body had been taken over by robots or aliens.

'You still there?'

'A cabin on Yellow Lake.'

'Which cabin?'

'About two miles from the Black Bear Tavern. There's a turning in the—'

'Junction of County D?'

Yes. Yes.

'Robinson place?'

Finally. *Yes*.

'Is that where you're calling from?'

Something was wrong. Something in the man's voice – that tinge of shrill tension – didn't quite fit.

'No.' Peter squeaked out the word – an obvious lie.

He looked out of the window. He recognized Charlie and the shovel boy, the one Etta said looked like a weasel. Jonah's chipmunk boy was there too. The fourth man – he was acting like the leader, so it must have been Kyle – put his hand in his pocket, pulled out his mobile, took a call. The others backed up and cocked their heads, listening. Then they looked at the cabin. It was as if they knew what Peter was doing inside, it was as if they were listening.

'So, you're not on the premises?'

'No.' Another squeak. 'I just saw, like I said, when I was driving by.'

The man's voice changed again, back to nice-guy uncle voice.

'Well, you know I don't think you got much to worry about. Probably just some hunters out setting bait for the bears.'

'They have guns. They have men tied up.' The words came out before Peter could stop them. 'I've seen them before. One guy's called Charlie.'

Another silence. Another crunch of metal from somewhere far away. Oh, Jesus. Why had he said that?

'So you *are* in the cabin?' Bye-bye, nice uncle, welcome back, RoboCop.

Peter didn't answer. Put down the phone, he told himself. Walk away from the phone.

He stayed on the line long enough to hear what came next. Something about how people had the right to shoot trespassers around here, and if something bad happened to him, it'd be his own goddamn fault.

Chapter Thirteen
—
ETTA

I stood next to the window beside the bed where Jonah was curled up like a baby, rocking back and forth.

I needed to pull the curtains open for a second – have a good look, find out what was going on outside, who was *really* there on the lawn – but my hands just wouldn't budge.

Jonah coughed and wheezed. Had he breathed in too much of that strange smoke? Weird noises – half sung, half said – came from the back of his throat and gurgled out like dark, boiling liquid.

Outside on the lawn, a car door slammed.

I touched the edge of the curtain.

Don't be such a chicken, Etta. Just look.

I turned it back an inch or two.

There. See? Blink, why don't you. Look again, just to make sure.

They were standing in front of Kyle's blue car,

exactly how I'd imagined them – Charlie the fat guy, the weasel boy, the other kid that Jonah said looked like a chipmunk. And Kyle, carrying a rifle. Not an old shotgun like Charlie's, but a skinny-barrelled black thing with a scope on the end.

I saw something else that I wasn't expecting. Four more men were sitting in the other car, totally still, not moving a muscle. I couldn't see their faces, but their stiff bodies looked like statues. I pushed the curtain back a little more to get a clearer look. What was it Kyle had said on the phone that time? 'We gotta show those Chicago guys we mean business.' Is that who those men were? The Chicago guys?

I closed the curtain. All of a sudden, it hit me – Kyle wasn't looking for me, after all. This was about something else – that powder on our kitchen counter, the crumpled-up money stacked up in a pile, those men in the car. Me, Peter, Jonah – we'd just picked the wrong cabin to hide out in, that was all. This was just a coincidence, some kind of sick joke.

Peter stumbled in from the living room. He was shaking all over – what the hell had happened out there? Hadn't he got through? Somehow he managed to turn the lock on the doorknob and close the door.

'The sheriff won't be coming to help us.' His voice

shook and his lips hardly moved while he croaked out the words. 'Nobody will.'

'What are you talking about?'

'They've got somebody in on it, whatever they're up to, Kyle and his gang. That fucking deputy – he told them we're here.'

On the bed, Jonah's chanting got louder. His breathing was off, too – raspy and shallow – like his lungs were filling up with water.

I looked outside. Kyle was looking straight at the cabin. He said something to the other men, and then he came loping toward the door with big arrogant strides.

'He's coming,' I said. 'We'll have to go through the windows, out the back way.'

I rushed across to the other side of the room, opened the windows and tried to unhook the rusty screens. 'Jonah's path to the lake – we can swim for it if we have to.'

Behind me, Jonah was still droning his weird song. Peter took my place at the curtains. 'Not a chance,' he said, numbly. 'He's already at the bloody door.'

'Come on, then.'

Peter didn't move.

'We can't give up now, can we? What's the matter with you?'

I managed to get one of the metal hooks unfastened, but the other one was fused to the window.

'Help me!' I screamed. Finally, Peter sprang into action. He crossed the room and pushed his shoulder against the screen, swearing non-stop, like that would make him stronger.

'Push,' I said.

Too late.

Kyle's hard-fisted knock on the front door shook the whole cabin.

Boom. Boom. Boom.

Peter stopped pushing. 'The bathroom,' he whispered. 'It's safe in there.'

The bathroom? Had he gone completely crazy?

He held my shoulders. 'Mum always said. In a tornado or a bad storm.'

'This isn't a tornado, Peter,' I said, pulling away. 'We've got to get out.'

'No. They'll catch us.'

'We'll be sitting ducks in there.'

'It'll be safer, OK? Another locked door.'

The pounding on the front door got louder. The men were shoving something against it – a board or a log. There was noise coming from the lake side, too, shattering glass, breaking windows. Someone was

on the porch, trying to break through the back door –
kicking at it, banging away.

'Let's push the beds over, Etta. Once they get inside,
that bedroom door won't hold.'

Jonah came out of his coma for a few seconds and
offered an unsteady hand. The three of us heaved the
beds on top of each other and shoved them against
the door. We turned the double bed on its side, stood
it against the window facing the lake. There was a
flimsy closet in a corner. That went against the other
window, held in place by a little armchair.

'Right, then,' Peter said. 'Let's get inside.'

He guided me into the bathroom and Jonah
shuffled in behind us. Peter switched the light on,
closed the shutter on the window, fastened the metal
hook.

'There,' he said. 'Safer for a while.'

It didn't feel that way. Even Peter didn't believe it,
the way he was shaking again. And Jonah? He was
more out of it than ever. His eyes were closed and
his body was moving slightly, like he was listening to
music that only he could hear.

Lucky for him, I thought, to be so zoned out, to not
know the cabin was being smashed to the ground, to
not hear—

'Hey in there! Anybody home?'

Kyle's voice was like an angry giant's. The words 'fee fie fo fum' ran through my mind. Peter laughed – was he thinking that too? He leaned against the door, taking in deep breaths – as if that could keep out the memory of the words that came next.

I smell the blood of an Englishman.

JONAH

He wasn't dreaming. He wasn't even asleep, although he wasn't entirely awake, either.

His prayers on the beach had finally been answered – he'd been transported to another world, a better place. So why did these white kids keep trying to lure him away from it, dragging him back to a reality where he didn't want to be?

The tiny room's stark fluorescent light blinded him – he had to get back to the dark again. Pulling away from the English boy, he stepped into the bathtub. It seemed soft, fluffy, like a cotton cocoon – but too glaring, too bright.

He squeezed his eyes shut, covered his face with his hands. The music in his head grew louder as voices – one, two, a whole choir – murmured their rhythmic chant. What was this song? He'd heard it before, hadn't he? Something his grandfather had sung to him when he was a baby – it must have been. A hymn, handed down from generation to generation.

He heard the others talking – the girl, the white boy – but he couldn't understand their words. The world of his mind got darker and darker until finally it was night, and there, before his eyes, a million stars danced across the sky in circular formation, twisting and swirling like whirlpools of light.

He was flat on his back, looking up, amazed. A vague memory crept into his awareness – a hot, sticky summer night, in his other world. He tried to shake it, but it wouldn't let go. He'd been out with friends, drinking beer in a park in South Minneapolis. A girl from school, the pretty one he never could quite erase from his memory, had brought a couple of joints with her. She had shared one of them with him, and together they lay down on the damp grass, laughing, kissing, holding each other tightly, rolling in the coolness of the dew. Then the girl made him stop.

'Look,' she had whispered. 'The sky.'

At first they'd both thought it was a trick of the light, or a bizarre shared hallucination. But slowly, through their dope-addled haze they realized what they were seeing – aurora borealis, Northern Lights. Traces of light like sheer green and white ribbon shimmered across the sky as gracefully as dancers. It was over in seconds, but the display seemed to last for days, a transforming vision that Jonah knew would never leave him and that he thought would bind him to the pretty girl forever.

It didn't, of course. He saw her again the next night, and night after night during the summer vacation. But every time she ignored him, pretended they had never touched, had never kissed, had never seen the image of a colorful god, vibrating in the sky.

Jonah blinked, and the harsh light burned.

He closed his eyes, forcing himself to stop thinking about *then*, about *there*. He focused on the words of the hymn he'd been hearing in his head, and squeezed his eyes tighter until the twirling stars appeared again. This was what he had been praying for. This vision, not the memory of a world that had treated him so badly, had left him abandoned by his friends, his family, his past, his culture.

Slowly, the stars stopped swimming. The sky he gazed at was still dark, but another image appeared, huge and glowing like an enormous golden moon. It was his grandfather as a young man, his braids glistening black, his skin smooth and unmarked. He was dressed in gold buckskin that was decorated with intricate embroidered designs. His headdress glowed, as if the beads and feathers were electrified.

Jonah didn't really remember his grandfather, had never even seen a picture of him. But he recognized him instantly, and when the face smiled down at him like a kindly god, Jonah smiled back.

He had prayed hard enough, he had sung long enough.

He had seen his vision. Now he would wait for guidance to come.

ETTA

One. Two. Three. . . Four!

I counted the bashes on the bedroom door. How long would the saggy mattress barricade hold them back? A minute, if we were lucky. And then—

'Etta?'

Peter held me by the shoulders. He was calmer now. The breathing must have worked – it had stopped the shakes, anyway.

'You were right,' he said. 'We should've run.' He glanced at the tiny bathroom window. 'Come on.'

He opened the hook and pushed out the shutter. The soft sunlight shone through – I'd forgotten it was still daytime. The air from outside was warm and inviting. The forest's edge was only a few feet away.

'Hurry, Peter!'

We heard the bedroom door come crashing down and an army of footsteps stomp across the wooden floor. I could feel myself panicking as the sounds got closer. I wanted to put my hands up to my mouth and scream my head off like they do in the movies.

But Peter stayed cool. He loosened the inner screen's hooks and banged on the wooden frame. Nothing. Stuck tight. He pushed and punched the rusted mesh. The metal scraped into his skin, bloodying his knuckles.

He pushed even harder, tearing his skin, swearing under his breath, a long stream of words that came out like Jonah's weird song.

Finally! The swearing must have done it! He tore a wide hole in the metal, ripping his skin.

'Go!' he whispered.

I shook my head and pointed at Jonah, who was swaying now, dancing to a song that only he could hear. 'We've got to get him out first.'

In the bedroom it got quiet. No footsteps, no pounding on the bathroom door. What was going on out there? I tried to listen for clues – breathing, whispers – but Jonah's mumbled song made it impossible.

'*I'll* get Jonah out,' Peter hissed. 'You've got to go *now*.'

Footsteps shuffled on the other side of the door. Something went *click*. Kyle's gun, I thought – maybe he was loading up his rifle, standing back a few feet, taking aim, getting ready to shoot us all, right through the thin plywood panels.

No, I thought. He'd never. . .

But Peter must have been thinking that too. His eyes were wide, like mine. He stared at the door, frozen with terror.

The footsteps creaked again. Somebody cleared his throat. We needed time – to wake Jonah up, to get through that window – but there wasn't any.

Unless. . .

I turned to the door.

You have to do this, I thought. There's no other way.

I took a deep breath.

Just say it.

'Kyle?'

I waited. No answer.

'Kyle. It's me, Etta.'

Peter looked at me like I'd lost my mind. I made waving motions, pointed at the bathtub where Jonah was sitting up, swaying from side to side, lost in his own world. Why didn't Peter understand what he needed to do – shake Jonah out of his stupor, or else haul him out the window by his arms or legs? Why didn't he realize that he had to go with Jonah, through the window, *right now*?

'Kyle, if you're out there, well, I just wanted to say that none of us is going to say anything about this to anybody.'

I held my breath, willing Kyle to answer.

Nothing. Then a rattle of the door handle.

'I mean, we ain't exactly *legal* here, if you know what I mean.'

Another rattle. A shove against the door.

'I 'spect I'm in a shit-load of trouble already, right? Huh, Kyle? Ain't I?'

What the hell was I doing? Talking like somebody on some talk show – who would *that* fool?

The door moved, groaning at the hinges as Kyle pressed his weight against it.

'The hell you doing here, girl?'

'Nothing, Kyle. We ain't doing nothing, like I said.'

'*Nothing, Kyle.*' His voice was mocking, sing-song. '*We ain't doing nothing.*'

I didn't say any more. There was more creaking wood as Kyle pressed harder on the door. I motioned to Peter. Come on, get moving.

'You might as well let us in,' Kyle rasped. 'You got nowhere to go.'

Finally, Peter was on his feet. He poked Jonah's

arm, shook his shoulders – no reaction.

'Right then,' he muttered, leaning over the tub, twisting on all the faucets.

As soon as the cold water hit him, Jonah jumped up, yowling in shock. He slipped on the wet enamel and bashed his head on the corner of the sink, opening a two-inch gash across his forehead. He put his hands up to the wound and wiped away the blood. Two red stripes were painted down each cheek. Like an Indian, I thought. A real live Indian, ready for war.

'Go!' I shouted, as the door behind me rumbled and began to splinter.

Peter climbed through first and pulled Jonah out with him. He dropped onto the soft sand and scrambled up again. Jonah had woken from his trance, his coma, whatever it was, and was moving away from the house. I clambered out after them, as the door came down. My foot caught the frame – the rusty screen cut a six inch slice across my ankle, and something twisted when I landed. Peter took my hand, helped me up, guided me back to the shelter of the forest.

JONAH

The water, the pain, the blood. What was going on? Jonah touched his stinging face and rubbed his eyes. Those crazy things he'd seen. Had he been dreaming or what?

He was back on solid ground – the red, sandy earth beside the cabin – being dragged into the woods. Etta hobbled beside him, wincing in pain as blood poured out of a cut in her ankle. Peter was in the lead, pulling them both towards the cover of trees, his eyes wide, his breathing frantic.

'Quick, run. . . I know where there's a path. Follow me.'

There were sounds inside the cabin – muffled shouts, crashing doors. The men. The fat guy with the shotgun, the bearded guy with the rifle – for a few blissful minutes, Jonah had forgotten about them.

'Hurry, Jonah. *Please.*'

Peter ducked to avoid the low branches and trudged into the undergrowth, Etta lagging behind him. She turned around and pleaded with Jonah, arms flailing.

'You've got to come before it's too late.'

They stood where his wigwam had been. Tramping the ground where he'd built his home. He looked into the woods – the cover of thick leaves, the impenetrable green lured him with promises of safety.

From inside the house somebody shouted, 'They're gone.'

Another voice. 'Where?'

'Don't know. Just ain't here.'

'The woods. Go get 'em.'

The front door of the cabin groaned open and slammed shut.

The men were back outside.

'Jonah. Please.' Etta was even more agitated now. The fear in her eyes burned him with shame – he'd seen that look before, in the wigwam, when he left her on her own.

'We've got to find the path,' Peter whispered.

They'd never make it through the forest, Jonah thought, not with Etta's hurt ankle. And Peter didn't *know* these woods – not like the gun guys who'd probably been hunting here for years and knew every dangerous dip, every fallen tree. If they all tried to run for it, they'd never stand a chance.

Jonah put his hands up, covered his face, breathed in the fragrant traces of the herbs. He could take those men out. Only two of them were armed. The odds weren't impossible. If he wanted it enough, he could.

If he prayed really hard.

What had happened after the fire on the beach today was *real*. He'd seen it, hadn't he? All that golden light. The spirits were there, waiting, ready to help him.

'Jesus, Jonah, come *on*.' Etta's cries were like a frightened animal's.

'Go,' he said, turning away from her, from them.

'The path,' Peter hissed. 'The path!'

Slowly, Jonah walked toward the front of the house. He heard Peter's shouts, Etta's cries, but he didn't listen.

He kept moving away. He had a *different* path to find.

ETTA

I watched Jonah disappear around the corner of the cabin. What was he doing? He was wobbling like a drunk – away from us, toward the men, singing that weird song he'd been mumbling in the tub. Why?

Peter couldn't see what was going on. He was still hunched down on the edge of the forest, half hidden behind a cluster of birch trees, ready to run for it. I was the only one who could see what Jonah was doing. I needed to stop him. I needed to drag him back to the woods before it was too late.

From the other side of the cabin one of the men shouted, 'Hey, Kyle. That Indian's still here.'

Come back, Jonah, I thought. Just come back.

From the corner of my eye, I saw Peter stumble out of the woods towards me.

'They'll find us any second,' he whispered. 'You've got to get help.'

He put his hands on my shoulders. His bright eyes gazed into mine, like he was trying to transfer some secret knowledge of the woods.

'Hurry, Etta. You'll make it to the Nussbaums's. I know you will.'

I looked down at the bleeding gash on my leg, felt the throbbing pain. There was no way I'd be able to plough through the thick undergrowth, not that far, anyway, and not that fast. Finally, I really *was* the injured girl in the movie who had to tell the others to go on without her. The only thing missing was the ripped prom dress.

'I can't run fast enough,' I said. 'You'll have to go.'

Peter looked deep into the woods, straining to glimpse the path. He turned to me, his face red and contorted.

'No,' he said, 'I'm not leaving you, and that's that.'

'But you're the only one who knows the way.' I gave his feet a gentle nudge to dislodge them. 'And I might be able to make Kyle see sense.'

He pulled me towards the woods again, shaking his head. 'If you're going to stay behind, you've got to hide. Go down to the lake. Away from the cabin.'

Out in the clearing, Jonah's singing got quieter. Slower.

We listened, holding our breath, until there was no sound except the cawing of a crow.

'We can't leave him,' I said.

'But promise me you'll stay hidden. Till I get back.'

I touched his arms, kissed his cheek. 'I promise. Now go!'

He thought for a second, then nodded in that funny, determined way he did when his mind was made up. And off he went, beating back branches with his bare arms, disappearing behind the thick green curtain that swayed in the wind.

JONAH

By the time he got to the front of the cabin, Jonah's head had cleared completely and he realized what a dumb-ass thing he'd done. There were no spirits hovering around him, ready to intervene in the world of mortals. There were just some white guys in front of a car brandishing shovels and guns.

Still, if they had to deal with him, they might leave Etta and Peter alone. It would buy them time. Stupid or not, maybe this wasn't such a bad idea.

'Hands up!' Charlie, the fat guy, shouted.

Jonah took a quick sniff of his palms, hoping he could conjure something with those herbs again. There was nothing mystical about his hands now, though. They were just filthy, smelling of sweat and ground-in dirt.

'You heard me, Injun. Top of your head.'

'OK.' Jonah placed his hands on his head, weaved his open fingers through his hair. 'I'm cool.'

'No you ain't, goddammit.' It was the skinny

chipmunk kid's turn to talk. 'You ain't cool one bit. You're trespassing, that's what you are. This ain't your goddamn property. It don't belong to you.'

Charlie turned and glanced nervously into the beaten-up white car. The tied up men were inside. They were blindfolded, but they moved a little – shoulders and heads – breathing, trembling. Jonah counted their shaded outlines – four. Four men plus me makes five, he thought. And there were only two guys standing in front of the car – the chipmunk kid and fat Charlie with the gun. Maybe he could rush them, catch them off guard, grab the gun before Charlie had time to shoot.

'Hey, Charlie!'

Too late. Kyle and the other kid, Weasel, came around the side of the cabin. Weasel was smoking a cigarette and Kyle balanced his rifle on his shoulder as if it were a cheap toy – a child's popgun or a plastic bow and arrow.

'Looks like you bagged yourself an Injun.'

Kyle and the weasel strode over to Jonah, stood so close he nearly gagged at the harsh fumes from the weasel's cheap smokes and the sour-smelling sweat patches on Kyle's denim shirt.

'Where's the girl?' Kyle barked.

Jonah looked at the ground. 'Dunno.'

He kept his head down, looked at his bare feet. Shoes would be good now, in case he got the chance to run. That gravel on the driveway would slow him right down. He remembered pictures he'd seen of elders walking over hot coals. Maybe he could pray again. If only he remember those words. He closed his eyes, concentrated.

He didn't see the punch that knocked him to the ground, but he felt it – a battering ram to the stomach that doubled him over, squeezed the air out of his body. He caught his breath, blinked a couple of times, saw the butt end of Kyle's rifle raised above him. He tried to roll away from it, but the rifle smashed down on his head like thunder. Things got dark for a second, but he fought to stay awake. He couldn't see anything but he remembered where he was, who he was, what was happening.

Get up, he told himself, as those prayers came back into his head.

Get up. Run. Away from the woods. Lure them away from Etta and Peter.

He struggled onto his knees. Kyle and the kid had their backs turned. Good. He could stand up now. He could run.

He got into a crouch. Everything was spinning. His head throbbed, his vision came and went in bright flashes, as if he were being struck by lightning over and over again.

On his feet. Walking. Moving. Praying. Another lightning crack. Another thunderous explosion.

The blast hurled him backwards, and as he fell he saw the smoke from the Kyle's gun. A hot light burned through the flesh on his shoulder. He wanted to cry out in pain, but before he could take another breath, the sky above him turned black. An eagle, huge and black, darkened the world with its massive shadow. It swooped down on Jonah and grabbed him in its claws. It flew off with him, far away, into a place of never-ending night.

PETER

He was nearly at the Nussbaum cabin when he heard the gunshot. Its thunder-crack chased him, the sound waves sent him sprawling out of the woods and tumbling onto the soft grass of the well-kept lawn.

He had to get up. There'd be another shot, any second now.

'For heaven's sake, Peter. *Get up*.' His mother's voice again, nagging him.

His mother? What was she doing here? She was dead, buried, in a cemetery far away in England. Why would she be at the Nussbaums's cabin telling a friend of hers that Peter was being childish again, being frightened again for no reason?

He really was losing it now, going mad with the fear.

Struggling to his feet, he stumbled onto the cabin's new cedar deck. As he got to the door a thin, white-faced woman slammed it shut with terrified force.

'I've already called the sheriff,' she shouted hysterically, 'so you better get the hell out of here, whoever you are.'

Somewhere in the house a baby was crying, an older kid, too. The TV was on, full volume, playing a whiney, cheesy song from some obnoxious cartoon.

'You hear me, buster – he'll be here any minute, mister, and I ain't kidding.'

Peter banged on the door. 'The next cabin over. Somebody's been shot. Get an ambulance. Tell them to hurry.'

He banged again. This woman wasn't Mrs Nussbaum, the kindly old neighbor he remembered, but where else could he go?

'Please? There are men with *guns*. Help us. *Please*.'

He slumped down on the deck and leaned against a rustic planter filled with bright red geraniums and blindingly yellow daisies. Beyond the nice lawn and flowers, beyond the locked door's green welcome mat with a picture of a black bear on it, beyond the thick, dark cloak of pines and birch and brush and oak, somebody was dying. He *knew* it.

Somebody was screaming. He *heard* it. Etta.

God, help her. Please. God. *Save* them.

He listened for a few seconds. The lady was on

the phone talking. Her voice was sweet and gentle, nothing like Mum's. But he still found it soothing, calming. He closed his eyes. He couldn't hear any sirens yet. How long would it take? Come on, lady, he thought. Stop rattling on.

Peter sat up, rubbed his head, slapped his face. Things around him were fading, as if someone, somewhere, were turning off the lights.

Come on, Peter.

He had to fight this exhaustion – take deep breaths, stay awake.

It was no use. Oblivion had found him. It was a huge bird hovering over him, using its sky-sized wingspan to make everything dark.

ETTA

I thought of Peter's words – *stay hidden* – but I couldn't help myself. I broke out of my hiding place in the woods and staggered into the clearing like a frantic, wounded deer.

'Jonah!'

He was sprawled on his back, his legs and arms spread out. Why was he just lying there? Why didn't he get up and run away?

I dropped to my knees beside him. I put my arms out to shake him awake but something was leaking on his shirt. It was wet and dark—

Blood? I pulled back my hands.

No. This can't be real.

The stain was spreading, soaking his shirt, forming a river that dripped onto the ground.

'You shot him,' I shouted. 'He's dying.'

My heart pounded and I couldn't breathe. Was I dying too? Everything was spinning – the gray gravel road, the faded green grass, the brown earth.

I put my hands on the ground to steady myself. I bent over Jonah's body and listened for the sound of breathing. Nothing.

'You killed him,' I sobbed, looking up at the men, wiping away the tears that made everything hazy. 'What did you have to kill him for?'

It was like they couldn't hear me. Fat Charlie stared at his gun. Chipmunk was behind the car, puking. Weasel smiled like a stupid stoner. I caught a glimpse of Kyle inside the car. He was sucking on a cigarette, blowing smoke through the open window, not even bothering to look out.

A gurgling sound came from the back of Jonah's throat. Still alive. I put my hand on the sleeve of his shirt, clutched the red-soaked material as if that could keep him with me. Maybe there was time. Maybe if somebody called an ambulance, he'd pull through.

'Please, please, won't you help us?' Fat rivers of snot and tears flowed down my face. I looked at the men again, tried to focus. Maybe one of them cared. The younger ones were like us. Just kids.

'*Please*. Before it's too late.'

They stood in front of the car in a jagged, blurry line. Charlie. Weasel. Chipmunk. Their faces were empty – blank white spaces. There was nothing in their eyes. No pity. No shame.

Jonah coughed. That meant he was still breathing, right? I touched his hair, felt his warm forehead. The blood wasn't coming out as fast, but it covered the front of his shirt now, and the pool on the ground was seeping into the dirt.

'Jonah?' I whispered. 'Can you hear me?'

He didn't answer. He didn't move. There was a sickening groan from the back of his throat, but after a few seconds that stopped, too.

I looked at the men again. Weasel lit up a cigarette, Charlie checked his watch. Nobody said anything. These guys were like soldiers, just doing their job. Nobody cared that Jonah was dying.

I shut up, too. What was the point of any more crying or pleading? I lay down next to Jonah, draped my arm across his body, closed my eyes and waited.

Part of my mind was still working, though. How could I get a gun or shovel out of somebody's hand? I pictured it – I'd jump up suddenly from where I was lying, take them by surprise. I'd kick Charlie in the nuts and grab his gun while he was bent over, then swing around and knock Kyle out with the gun-barrel.

But most of my mind was still, and that stillness slowed the frantic parts down, made them fade away, until I felt peaceful, almost happy.

I wasn't thinking at all, but hazy pictures floated in and out of my brain, like a pretty slide show. Mom was in some of them, laughing with me, holding my hand, kissing me. My brothers were there too, playing with me like they did when I was little – itsy-bitsy spider and peek-a-boo. A picture from one of the Duchess's fancy art books drifted past, one of a girl standing in a muddy creek, laughing, with her white skirt held up to her thighs. And the Duchess was sitting beside me on her expensive leather couch, pointing things out in the picture to me, saying she always knew what a smart girl I was. So smart, she said, the way I could always figure things out.

A car door slammed, jerking me back to reality. I opened my eyes a little, watched my right hand move up and down on top of Jonah's chest.

Up and down? Was he breathing? I listened. I could hardly hear but there it was – a tiny, wheezy snore.

I wanted to shake him awake but something hard and leathery touched my other hand. It was like the heel of a boot tapping on my skin, tickling me. Was this some kind of game?

Stay still, I told myself. Play dead. Blank everything out.

The boot – or whatever it was – pressed down harder, twisted back and forth. I held my breath, trying not to cry or shout, but it ground my hand into the dirt, and I felt the weight of it crunching my bones.

'You like that, Etta?' Kyle's voice. He pressed down harder. The flesh on my fingers tore. I bit my lips, squeezed my eyes shut so the tears wouldn't come out. Just get it over with, I thought, whatever you're going to do. I'm not going to beg again. I don't even care any more, so why don't you just. . .

Kyle took his foot away. I let out little breaths, imagined the cool air on my raw, burning skin.

'Let's see if the Injun's awake.'

I heard a dull thud. Jonah groaned in pain.

'Stop it,' I whimpered. 'Don't hurt him any more.' I wanted to get up, fight back, but my body was frozen and so was my brain. I was in a kind of cocoon. It was light blue, a nothing color. Empty.

'You say something, Etta?' Kyle, bending over me. 'Can't hear you from down there.'

He grabbed my wrist and yanked me up so hard my arm nearly came out of its socket. The rifle that was strapped across his back slipped a little, so he hiked it up with a twitch of his shoulder. He turned toward the woods. 'We got a couple more for you, Charlie.'

I looked over, blinked a few times to make sure I was seeing things right. There were the tied-up guys from inside the car, huddled together in a clearing, wearing blindfolds. Fat Charlie had a gun pointed to one guy's head.

A couple more. That meant Jonah and me.

Things went spinny again – my stomach heaved, my heart pounded. I had to find that cocoon again – the blue, empty place.

'It didn't have to be like this, Etta.'

Kyle's voice sounded echoey and far away, like he was talking down a hollow tube. He was right next to me, though, touching my hair, like that was supposed to reassure me. Like that was his way of saying sorry or something.

'It still don't have to, if you know what I mean.'

I straightened up, quick as I could. I moved away from him, but he stepped towards me again, even closer.

'Well?' he said.

Well what? What was he talking about?

'OK, then,' he sighed. 'Let's get this over with.'

He nodded to Weasel, who leaned over and

hoisted Jonah up by the shoulders, hauling him across the lawn like a bag of garbage, towards the woods where Charlie was waiting.

'No,' I shouted. 'Let him be.'

Weasel kept going. I tried to squirm out of Kyle's grip but he had both of my arms pinned tight to my body.

'Like I said, Etta, it's up to you.'

'Make him stop!'

Kyle ran one of his hands across my shoulder, up to my neck, touching the back of my ear with his fingers.

'That's what you want?'

'Yes,' I said. He tickled the back of my ear with his fingers. He made gentle tracing movements, around my ear, behind it.

'You sure?'

In my ear.

'Course I'm sure. Leave him alone.'

Kyle dog-whistled Weasel, nodded toward the ground. Weasel dropped Jonah and stood over his body, like he was waiting for Kyle to bark out the next order.

'OK, then,' Kyle said, smiling. He took my face, tilted it up by the chin. A brown spot of tobacco was stuck between two of his teeth.

'Let's go inside.'

Inside?

'What do we need to go inside for?'

Kyle pushed me toward the cabin, squeezing my arms, making the old bruises hurt again. 'And there's your mom always saying what a smart girl you are.'

My mom. Jesus.

'Don't do nothing till we're done,' Kyle shouted to the weasel.

Done? My stomach flipped over, bringing burning liquid to the back of my throat. I had to get away from him, away from the cabin door that was getting closer and closer.

'No good changing your mind now,' Kyle said.

My legs buckled and my feet dragged on the ground.

'Come on, Etta,' Kyle said, as he pulled me through the bashed-in door. 'It'll be fun.'

PETER

'You that boy from the Robinson place?'

Everything was hazy, as if somebody had wrapped his eyes in cling film. A man in uniform stood on the porch and looked down on him – a tall deputy sheriff in a brown peaked hat and tight-fitting brown jacket and trousers. The woman from the house was there too, clutching a heavy red blanket.

'Son? Can you hear me?'

Peter recognized the man's voice from the phone. He sounded like the first guy, whatever his name was. Johnson, that was it – the nice, helpful bloke.

'We got a patrol car on the way there now.'

Peter looked at the cop and shook his head. 'It'll be too late,' he said. He put his head down, wrapped himself with his arms and sobbed.

The fucking cabin, he thought, that fucking jealousy and pride. It was too late for anything now, too late for being sorry, too late for. . .

A patrol car. Shit.

That dodgy cop.

Peter looked up, wiped his eyes, his nose.

'Hey, officer?'

He wanted to shout, but the words came out in a croaky whisper. The deputy was lighting a cigarette, nodding along to the hawk-like screeches that came from his walkie-talkie. The woman put the blanket around Peter's shoulder as he tried to sit up.

'He wants to say something, Ray.'

'Don't send any cars,' Peter croaked.

The deputy flicked his cigarette away. He sat on the steps, his long legs spread apart in a macho pose. 'What did you say?'

Peter looked at the woman, who wrapped the blanket tightly as if she were trying to cocoon him, to keep him safe as well as warm. Her eyes were blue, like Mum's. They were wet and teary, as if she felt sorry for him, but she was nodding, smiling a little, encouraging him to speak.

'What's your name, honey?' she asked him.

'Peter.'

'Well, Peter, my name's Julie and this here's Ray. Now, I've known Ray for as long as I can remember. He goes to my church – every Sunday, never misses. And I would gladly swear on a stack of bibles that

Ray Bryson's a guy you can trust with your life.'

The deputy moved a little closer, bent down, leaned in.

'You wanna tell me what happened, son?'

'OK.' In a strange monotone voice that he scarcely recognized as his own, Peter told them about his journey to the cabin, about the girl who'd tumbled out of the darkness, and the Indian boy who built his own wigwam on Ojibwe land. He started to tell them the rest of the story, about the gun and shovel guys smashing down the doors...

Bryson? Is that what she said? Jesus Christ. *Bryson.* Wasn't that RoboCop's name?

'Well?' Bryson took off his hat and ruffled a thick, sandy mop of hair. His eyes narrowed and he started twitching his fingers, running his thumbs along the side of his hat.

'Come on, son. You can tell me.'

There it was – the change in his voice. Impatience. Irritation. Harshness, like scraping on metal.

'There's nothing,' Peter said, his throat hoarse, his mouth desperately dry. 'Sorry. I heard a gun go off. That's all I know.'

'Okey-doke, then.' The nice cop voice was back again. Maybe Peter had got this all wrong. Maybe this *was* the good guy. 'I'll head over. See if they need backup.'

The deputy strutted back to his car. He turned on the red and blue and yellow lights, but left the siren off. From inside the car he waved to Peter and smiled at Julie. He started up the engine, tipped his hat to the child in the doorway, and silently pulled away.

Julie went to the open door. 'Come on inside, Peter,' she said. 'Have something to eat.'

'In a minute, if you don't mind.'

As soon as the door was closed behind her, Peter got on his feet and let the blanket drop to the floor. He shook out his arms and legs, tiptoed across the deck.

This was stupid, he thought. Julie went to *church* with the guy. How bad could he be?

Inside the kitchen, Julie rattled pans and hummed to herself. After a second or two, a light came on – soft and golden – an invitation to shelter, safety, a hot, tasty meal.

'Come on, Peter.'

He ducked below the window level. When he was sure Julie couldn't see him, he jumped off the deck and sprinted across the lawn to the edge of the woods. It was darker now – he could hardly see the path. He dived in, anyway, pushing forward, as if the forest

were a huge, stormy sea, and as if Etta were out there
somewhere – sinking, drowning – and only he could
pull her back to land.

ETTA

'You need to get washed up.'

Kyle pulled me toward the kitchen sink, stuck my cut, swollen hand under the faucet. The water still worked – it felt nice and cool on my burning hand – but everything else in the kitchen was wrecked. Drawers were hanging out, those pretty yellow dishes had been smashed on the floor, the telephone wires stuck out of the wall like plastic neon veins.

Outside the window I could still make out the narrow strip of lawn and the thick, dark wall of forest – our hiding place on the first night. Maybe I could get back there – it was only thirty feet away – smash the window, dive out. There wasn't a path like there was on the other side of the cabin, but I could drag Jonah into the undergrowth, find someplace safe until Peter came back.

'Your face, too.' Kyle turned the water off, pulled me up close to him again. 'I want you looking clean.'

He picked up a damp, stinky rag from the bottom

of the sink. He put some dishwashing detergent on it, rubbed it hard across my face until I had to spit out the suds.

'There,' he said when he was finished. 'All pretty.'

He touched the side of my face and smoothed my hair. 'When we're done, I'll let you and the Indian kid go.' He was talking softly now, nice and sweet, like I was his girlfriend.

'Them spics in the woods, too – all we wanted to do was scare 'em, so they'd stop muscling in on our business.'

Lies. I knew that. But I nodded my head, smiled. I had to keep him going like this, play dumb, just like Mom would. If he thought I believed the crap he was talking, maybe he'd let his guard down, drop the gun, give me the chance to run away.

'Long as you promise,' I said. That was good, wasn't it, stringing him along?

Kyle led me into the living room with his arm around my shoulder, like this was *his* cabin now and I was getting the grand tour. It didn't look like a cabin any more, though. It was like a bomb had gone off – torn curtains, the table split in two, pieces of shattered glass from the broken window sprayed across the floor.

Kyle set me down on the couch next to the fireplace. He took his rifle off, like a cowboy in a movie, leaning it against the sofa, facing upwards.

'There we go,' he said. 'Nice and cosy.'

He stood in front of me, bending down so his knees brushed against mine. He moved them backwards and forwards so they touched me for a second, then didn't touch. He rocked his hips a little – touching, not touching.

'Or maybe you want it in the bedroom?'

It. My stomach heaved again. I kept my eyes down, thought about something else so I wouldn't get sick. I concentrated on the braided rug in front of the fireplace. The colors were so pretty – brown, gray, red.

Kyle sat next to me and put his outstretched hand on my bare thigh.

'Well? Where's it gonna be?'

I looked out the broken window, the shards of glass like razor-sharp teeth. What difference would it make, I thought – here or there? This room or that room? The cabin or the woods or the lake? Any place, any time – it was all going to end up the same way.

Then I remembered the morning – the sweet, yellow light when I woke up, the peaceful sounds of Peter asleep, the gentle lapping of the waves on the shore, like a lullaby coming through the window.

'Not the bedroom,' I said.

'Right here, huh?' Kyle put his arm around my waist, squeezing me, moving his hands up along my side, my front. 'Sounds good to me.'

I tried to twist my body to get his hands away, but he grabbed my hair and before I could even breathe, he'd straddled me with his legs, pinning me underneath him. I couldn't move any more, couldn't wriggle away, couldn't do anything to stop him from—

Lights. Colors dancing across the walls, reflecting off the shattered glass. Yellow, red, blue.

Kyle got up, grabbed his gun. 'Down,' he barked. 'Now.'

I dropped to the floor and curled up into a little ball, with my legs tight together, my arms wrapped around my body.

What was out there? An ambulance? The cops? It had to be, with lights like that. Peter must have gotten through.

Oh, thank you, Peter. Thank you, thank you.

I tried not to shout. I had to keep calm, stay cool. If I was quiet enough, still enough, maybe Kyle would forget I was here and when he went out to see who it was I could—

A car door slammed. Footsteps came towards the cabin.

'Hey!' A man's voice through the kitchen door. The sheriff, had to be. Or a paramedic.

I took a deep breath and put my good hand to my mouth. No screaming. Not yet. There could be an ambulance outside. Right this minute they might be loading Jonah onto a stretcher, giving him fresh blood, getting ready to take the bullet out and stitch up the hole. I had to give them time to get away. When they started the engines and turned on the sirens, I could shout for help then.

'You OK in there?' The man's voice again.

Don't answer. Just listen.

He said something else that I couldn't make out, and another man – it sounded like the weasel – started to laugh.

Something wasn't right. Why would a paramedic be cracking jokes?

Kyle looked down at me and smiled. 'Everything's fine and dandy in here, Sheriff,' he said.

Sheriff. How did he know?

'Okey-doke,' the man outside said. 'Just checking, Kyle.'

My stomach twisted up, like a hand was inside

me, pulling at my guts.

Kyle. Sheriff. Somebody *was* in on it – Peter was right. So there wasn't any ambulance outside, wasn't going to be one, ever. And nobody was coming to help us, because nobody even knew we were here.

They probably got Peter on his way to the Nussbaums's.

Jonah would just keep bleeding, if he wasn't already dead.

'Right,' Kyle said. 'Let's hurry this up.'

And then it would be me.

PETER

The forest slowed him down – thick-bodied trees muscled in front of him, vines grabbed his feet, and finally, the earth's dips and troughs trapped his legs, sent him sprawling, roughing him up with sharp twigs and jagged stones.

He was laid out flat on his face, winded, sweating. In front of him, just beyond the edge of the woods, was the cabin and a shiny cop car parked in front, spewing out light. Bryson stood beside it, talking to the fat bloke with a gun, and the skinny weasel kid, having a right laugh about something. Peter wanted to cry – why had he let that bastard get a head start? If he'd taken off from the Nussbaums's sooner, Bryson would have chased him through the woods on foot and then. . .

What was that on the ground?

Peter remembered the shot, Etta's scream.

It was Jonah, face down, arms outstretched, legs sprawled out, like something on the ten o'clock news. And there was Bryson – a cop, for Christ's sake –

laughing and joking as if it were nothing, as if *Jonah* were nothing.

But where was Etta? Peter scanned the clearing – Bryson, lighting a cigarette, Weasel, standing with his hands folded across his chest, Charlie waddling back toward the woods.

But no Etta. And no Kyle.

'Hey,' Bryson shouted. 'How long does it take you?'

Who was he talking to? How long did *what* take? Peter listened for an answer, his heart pounding. Everything was quiet, except for the razor-sharp squawks of a blackbird.

'Seriously, dude.' Bryson took a step toward the cabin, as though he were talking to somebody inside. 'I'm sure she's a little honey, but can't you make it quicker?'

Kyle was in the cabin. He had to be. And the *she*? The *honey*?

What was going on in there?

Peter inched his body closer to the edge of the forest, trying to push Bryson's filthy words out of his head. He couldn't think now, he just had to get to the cabin, find some way to get Etta out of there, away from Kyle, away from whatever disgusting thing he was planning to do.

Bryson flicked his cigarette onto the lawn.

'I mean it, Kyle. We got shit to do here. If you ain't outta there in five minutes, I'm coming in after you.'

Peter crouched behind a hollowed-out log. Bryson and Weasel were both looking towards the woods. He'd have to go now, while they were distracted, before the five minutes were up. Against Kyle he might have a chance – if Etta hadn't been hurt too badly, it'd be two against one, but if Bryson went into the cabin. . .

Bryson turned to the car. Weasel wandered towards the forest.

This was his chance – he got up onto his feet and raced toward the cabin, crouching down as soon as he got to the front, ducking below the windows so that no one could see him. He sat still. Listened for sounds inside.

Weird, how quiet it was. No screams, no whispers, no shoving or struggling or. . .

Maybe he'd got this wrong. Maybe the whole thing was a set-up, a trap. Bryson must have known he'd run back to the cabin. Were those horrible things he said about Etta just bait?

Peter's breathing got heavier, and his hands trembled. No. He couldn't start shaking now. He had to calm down. Trap or not, it didn't matter. Jonah's body on the lawn was real enough. Those tied-up guys he'd seen in the car, they were real. Etta was in danger – *real danger.* He had to go in. Now, while there was time. Now, while there might be a chance.

He crawled towards the porch and crept up the stairs. The back door was smashed in, shattered. Peter looked through the jagged slats, but he could only make out vague outlines – the couch, the dining table, the square of dusky light that came through the kitchen window, the flickering lights of the cop car dancing across the walls.

The door groaned as he opened it, the bottom edge scraped along the porch. Whoever was inside knew he was coming. If this was an ambush, he was walking right in and shouting a big halloo.

It took a few seconds for his eyes to adjust to the dark. He straightened up and took a deep breath. He smelled something – that strange smoke Jonah had burned on the beach. He breathed in again. . .

There – on the floor, in front of the fire, half hidden by the sofa.

He blinked and squinted, straining to see.

An outstretched arm. A leg. A pool of something dark and nasty.

Another body. What have they done?

He walked across the floor. He felt cold – not on his skin, but inside, as though something had iced up his heart and lungs and all the muscles and bones that held them in place. Barely breathing, he stumbled closer. The blinking lights made everything look out of joint – the foot on the body seemed huge, the leg was too long, the arm was thick, heavy.

'Peter?'

The voice was tiny, trembling. Peter's heart kicked into action again – Etta. Christ, it was Etta. What the hell was happening here?

'I thought you were dead, Peter,' she said.

She was hunched over on the step that led to the bedroom. She was holding onto something – a massive, black gun – clutching it to her chest as if she were clinging to a tree against a rushing torrent of water.

'I thought they killed you.' Her voice was calm and her face was still, but the rest of her body quivered dangerously. Peter took her hands, unfolded them and released the gun that was covered in sticky blood and clotted hunks of hair and skin. He leaned it against the fireplace and looked down.

There was Kyle – on his side, motionless.

'He was trying to take my bra off,' Etta said, blankly. 'I think I killed him.'

She poked Kyle's body with one of her toes. 'See?'

Peter leant down and touched Kyle's chest. 'I guess I shouldn't have bashed him so many times,' Etta said. 'After he was on the floor, maybe I should have just stopped, but—'

'He's still breathing,' Peter whispered. 'We've got to go now before he wakes up, or before the others come in.'

Suddenly, Etta stood up, her hands fluttering in front of her face like a bird's wings. Peter took her by the shoulders and set her gently her back down. They had to keep still. They were nearly safe now – they had Kyle's gun. All they had to do was keep quiet, find a place to hide – get down to the lake or into the thick woods.

'Jonah,' she whispered.

On the floor in front of them, Kyle's legs twitched. He let out a moan, then settled again.

It was then that Peter saw the phone in Kyle's back pocket. He carefully dug it out with his fingers. Kyle didn't move or make any noise. Peter turned the phone on, watched it light up, the signal bars climbing up the side.

'Take this.' He handed Etta the phone. 'Take this, and call 911. Ask for an ambulance. Tell them everything, if you want – what happened, where we are – but most of all, we need an ambulance for Jonah. Can you do that?'

Etta looked at him, nodded purposefully.

Then he picked up the gun. The sleek barrel, the smooth solid metal, frightened him. How could something designed to give him power make him feel so weak?

He gave it back to Etta. 'Take this, too.' He was glad to be rid of the horrible thing. 'Go down to the lake – find a hiding place in the woods, where we first saw Jonah.'

She was about to protest but Kyle groaned again, like a hibernating animal returning to life.

'I'll get Jonah, Etta. You've got to stay safe.'

He took her hand, guided her across the minefield of shattered glass and coaxed her through the door, helping her down the porch's steps. He stood on the lawn and watched her tread carefully down the hill, holding the gun as far from her body as she could. She stopped for a second and looked back up at him. Then she was gone, safe in her haven of bushes and trees.

Right then, Peter thought.

He crept along the side of the cabin, flattened his body against the wall, inched past the bedroom window, the kitchen window. When he got to the front of the cabin, he peered around the corner. There was Jonah – halfway between the cabin and the parked cars. There was Bryson, close to the edge of the woods, smoking a cigarette, watching something that was going on in the forest.

Peter took a deep breath. How many steps would it take to get to Jonah's body? Eight or so. Then he'd have to drag him to the woods on the other side of the cabin. How far was that? Thirty meters? He could do that, couldn't he? Of course. As long as he had enough adrenaline pumping – and as long as Jonah didn't wake up and start shouting in pain.

Right then. That bloody phrase again.

Without thinking any more, he took off running, silently counting off the seconds with each step – one thousand one, one thousand two. When he got to Jonah's body, he was already at seven. He glanced up. Bryson was still puffing away, oblivious.

He bent down and took hold of Jonah's arms under the shoulders. Jesus, there was so much blood. The wound was huge – red and gaping, like a horrible mouth.

Don't look at it, Peter. Don't think. Just get on with it.

He twisted Jonah's body, rolled him onto his back. He held him under the shoulders, pulled as hard as he could. No good – Jonah's shirt ripped. He had to bend down further, get a proper grip.

Right. Now try again. Hang on tight. That's it.

They were moving – one foot, two feet, three. He looked up again. He was nearly around the side of the cabin now. A few more feet and he'd be out of Bryson's line of sight.

'Hey!'

Bryson was shouting.

Don't stop, Peter.

'Hey guys, get back!'

Had Bryson seen him?

Peter kept pulling. Just bloody get on with it!

Closer to the woods. He glanced backwards. Closer. He didn't look at anything except Jonah's shirt – at the wound getting bigger, wetter, bloodier.

His heart pounded, his back was breaking, his lungs burned.

Keep going, son. Good lad.

He felt something sharp on his back – the branch of a pine tree. He hunched over Jonah's body, protecting it from the pointed thrusts of broken twigs and the cat's claw scratches of brambles and burrs. He bent down even lower – on his knees now – and pulled, pulled, pulled. The dark undergrowth got thicker, spread over him like a rough blanket, cutting out light.

He was going into the woods – deeper, deeper – until he couldn't go any further. No more strength to push his back beyond the thick shrubs, or to pull poor Jonah another inch.

He stopped, listened. He couldn't see the front lawn from here – the cars, the men. They must have noticed that Jonah's body was gone by now. They'd be looking, following the trail of blood, straight to where he was hiding.

He listened for their grunts, their footsteps.

All he could hear was Jonah's rattly breath.

'Not long now, mate,' he whispered.

Not long for what?

Peter knew the answer, but he didn't care any more. When the men came, when they shot him and Jonah, at least somebody would live – Etta would survive.

'That's some consolation, isn't it, mate?'

He closed his eyes – so tired now. He wished he

could pray. But he could only think about Mum, imagine her on that daft fluffy cloud, waiting for him, getting impatient, telling him to hurry it up, to get a move on, to *listen to her*, for goodness' sake.

He opened his eyes – had he been sleeping? He listened.

Sirens. Cars. Voices – women and men. It was as if a huge army were forming out on the lawn – a massive chorus of barking commands.

And there were colors through the trees, lighting up the sky as if it were Bonfire Night – swirling orbs of red, yellow, white, blue, as the cop cars and the ambulances covered the lawn, making an impenetrable web out of metal and wheels.

He sat still and crossed his legs, letting Jonah's head rest in the hollow of his lap. He put his head down and listened to Jonah's chest. Up, down. In, out. Wheeze, hiss.

He could stop being afraid now.

Job done, he thought, hearing Dad's voice in his head. Job bloody well done.

Car doors slammed. Ambulance engines roared. Through the dense trees he saw Etta limping up the hill towards him, both arms waving, no sign of the gun.

'Hey,' she shouted, peering into the brush. 'Where are you guys?'

Carefully, Peter set Jonah on the ground and stood up. He pushed away the scrub to clear a path. When Etta emerged through the undergrowth, he reached out for her and she took his hand. Together, they crawled out of the woods and walked arm in arm – away from the dark, away from the fear – up the hill to the shining lights.

Chapter Fourteen
—
JONAH

All in all, being dead wasn't so bad. There were no white lights, the black eagle had gone. There was just a slow, gray dimming, and Jonah hovered above the ground on a cool, wet cloud.

Gradually, the cloud grew warmer. Something soft was put over his body, thawing his frozen limbs, making them shake violently as they were gently coaxed back into a harsh and painful life.

He was aware of sounds, horrible beeping, shallow, wheezy breath – his own.

Jonah moaned, semi-conscious, opening his eyes to a noisy, blurry world.

'He's awake again.'

Not for long, Jonah thought. Not if I can help it, anyway.

The pain was duller than it had been before – a nagging, persistent ache. It was hard to breathe, too. He had to force himself to move his chest up and down, in and out, in time with the beeps. It took so long, though. Breathe in slowly . . . wait . . . out. . .

Was that enough? Was he taking in enough oxygen to keep himself alive?

He looked around. A white, windowless space, a wall that supported the labyrinth of tubes attached to his body. A hospital room. No, the ceiling was too close to his head. An ambulance, that was it.

'You must be Jonah.' A woman in a green jacket, with curly reddish hair was sitting at his feet – a female leprechaun, but taller, and without the hat and pipe. 'Jonah? Is that right?' Her voice was soft, calm. She wasn't scared or panicky. She was just doing her job.

He felt himself nodding. God, it was hard work.

'Can you wiggle your toes for me, Jonah?'

He could, a little.

'Can you wave your fingers?'

That was easier.

'Right now, what we're doing is we're waiting here until a helicopter comes so we can take you to the Cities. We don't have the right equipment to take care of you up here, so we're gonna fly you over to Minneapolis. Doctors are waiting there to operate on you.'

Operate?

He heard the beeps get faster. Memories seeped into his brain. Blurred images faded in, out – a face above his. The last things he remembered – hitting the ground, pain, like fire, a face looking down on him – *Etta's* face.

'Keep breathing, Jonah.'

He moved his mouth. He had to talk. Up and down – that was good. See? He could talk and breathe at the same time. He swallowed. His mouth was dry and tasted of straw. He moaned softly, half-humming, half-grunting the word. 'Etta.'

'Oh, she's fine. The other kid, too. Everybody's just fine. Nobody died.'

Jonah imagined that he was nodding. Good. Good. Better now.

He closed his eyes. His vision went funny again – the painkillers doing their trippy stuff. He saw sweeping lights across a midnight-blue sky – green, yellow – behind them a bright face, getting bigger, huge as the heavens. Two black eyes shining – wet with tears.

His mom?

He needed to call her. Now. She'd be panicking, worried sick. He had to let her know where he was

– *right* now – explain everything that happened, tell her that. . .

The beeping got faster, louder. The paramedic jumped out of her seat, grabbed something, shoved it onto Jonah's mouth like a muzzle.

'Jonah, you need to calm down,' she said softly, keeping a firm grip on the suffocating mask. 'Come on now, take deep breaths.'

He wanted to pull it off, kick her away from him, but there was something in her voice that made him obey.

'In. Out. You can do it.'

The beeping slowed down. The paramedic loosened her hold on the mask. After a few seconds, she attached it to his ears with two stretchy cords. That was better, Jonah thought, easier, with the mask on. Easier without fighting against it. Easier letting this nice lady help.

The colors were coming back, pink and silvery when he closed his eyes. He heard his mother's voice, softly singing. He felt her hand on his forehead, her fingers through his hair.

'My mother,' he croaked. 'You need to call my mom.'

Then he drifted off again, to a happier sleep.

ETTA

The grown-ups were back in charge. Dozens of them swarmed on the front lawn – FBI agents, paramedics, people wearing space suits used for decontaminating chemical spills. Lights – cherry red, neon blue, electric white – danced on the roofs of cars and trucks and ambulances. I watched all the action from the bedroom window while I waited for some people in suits – social workers, I figured – to get done talking to Peter so they could interview me.

Outside on the lawn, an ambulance crew was taking care of the men who'd been hauled into the woods. They were kids, really, same as the guys in Kyle's gang. One of them couldn't stop shaking. A lady was talking to him, trying to calm him down, while a man reached into his bag and took out a needle. When the kid saw it he panicked, yelled out something in Spanish, squirmed like a cat in a plastic bag about to get drowned. The jab in his arm put an end to all that squawking, of course. Bringing somebody down didn't take very much effort – a needle, a gunshot, a bash to the skull.

I hadn't killed anybody, though. Even with the blood and skin torn off, all I'd done to Kyle was give him bad concussion. By the time the cops cuffed him, threw him in the back of a car and drove him away with the rest of his gang, he was wide awake, complaining about police brutality, threatening to sue.

But killing was easy. I'd never known that before. A little more muscle, a better aim, one or two more whacks – that's all it would've taken.

'Etta? Can we talk to you?'

One of the social workers came into the room with two chunked-up state troopers. She was wearing a beige suit and flat shoes. Her hair was short and brown with bits of gray in it, so it looked the same color as her clothes.

'You're not in any trouble, Etta.' The woman's voice was all sing-song and sweet. I imagined Mom, rolling her eyes, making that two-fingers-down-your-throat gagging sign. 'Like we said to your friend Peter, we just need to check a few things out.'

The woman sat down on the bed that I'd slept in and motioned for me to sit down on the other.

'Whatever.'

I pushed the other bed as far back as I could. The two cops stood in front of the door, like they were guarding it.

'Right, Etta.' The lady looked up from the clipboard she was holding. 'We have those men in custody, so nobody can hurt you.'

'Good,' I said. I felt my nose tingle, the tears welling up. I didn't want to cry – not in front of *her* – so I looked at the floor. There was a little rug between the beds, a braided one, like the one in the living room, the one I had looked at when Kyle was trying to—

'Were you assaulted by Kyle Boyer, Etta?'

Assaulted. That didn't sound so bad.

'Were you *sexually* assaulted?'

I took in a deep breath. I tried to, anyway, but my throat closed up like somebody had sucked the air from my lungs and filled them up with hunks of snot.

'Etta?'

I coughed and choked, nodded towards the uniformed guys.

'Can you get them out of here?'

The woman looked at the men and they lumbered back into the living room.

325

'That's better,' she said. 'Now can you tell me what happened, Etta?'

'What you said. That's what he wanted to do, that's what he *tried*. . .'

All the time I was talking, the woman wrote things down.

'Go on.'

I didn't want to give any of the details – not to her.

'That's why I bashed him on the head, OK? To stop him.'

'Etta, I already told you. *You're* not in any trouble.'

She straightened her back, put her pen down.

'Do you know why Kyle was so interested in this cabin?'

I shook my head.

'Were you aware he was involved with drugs?'

I shrugged.

'You need to answer the question, Etta.'

'The night he took me, I saw some stuff, some powder.'

'Where did you see it?'

My heart pounded. I couldn't lie – that would be a crime, right? But if I told the truth, what would happen to Mom?

'Did you see it here, in the cabin?'

I shook my head again, looked back down at the floor.

'Look, Etta, I'll get straight to the point. Did your mother know that Kyle was setting up a methamphetamine lab?'

'What?'

'Kyle Boyer moved from the Milwaukee area at the same time you and your mother got here from Minnesota. We're trying to work out if that's just a coincidence.'

'Of course it is,' I said.

'Are you positive on that?'

'Of course I am.'

The drugs on the counter. Methamphetamine. Jeez, Mom.

The tears welled up again. The woman reached into the pocket of her suit jacket and took out an unopened packet of tissues. She must have known I'd cry. She must have bought them special, just for me.

I wiped my snotty nose with the bottom of my top.

'No thanks,' I said.

There were more questions about what happened that night in the car – who was driving, which guy was sitting where. There were questions about Mom

– how long had she known Kyle? Where did they go when they went out on dates?

I just kept shrugging. I didn't know the answer to any of her questions. By the time she was finished, I wasn't even listening, I couldn't even hear.

Finally, she put away her pen and made the papers in her clipboard nice and neat.

'Right,' she said, with that sickening smile on her face again. 'One last question.'

I stood up, crossed my arms – this was taking way too much time.

'Do you *want* to go back home with your mother, Etta?'

'What?' I said.

'If you don't want to, we can arrange—'

'Course I do.' I said it as fast as I could, so she wouldn't be able to finish her sentence.

'You're sure?'

'Course I'm sure.'

The lady stood up. 'OK,' she said, standing in the doorway. 'I got my answer. I had to ask.'

After she was gone I went to the other side of the room and looked out at the lake. It was quiet this side, peaceful. The lake was a deep slate-blue color, but tiny traces of sunset still glimmered on the surface of the water. I heard footsteps behind me, a knock on the wall where the bedroom door had been.

Now what did she want?

'Etta?'

I turned around. *Peter.* He'd wet his hair down and washed off some of Jonah's blood. His shirt was still stained, though, and his arms and legs were dirty from hiding in the woods.

He came into the room, shaking his head at the sight of the overturned furniture and broken windows, like it was all coming back to him, like the whole scene was playing over in his head.

'They told me I could have a wash, get cleaned up a little, before. . .'

'Before what?' I asked.

Peter shrugged, but I'd known as soon as I opened my mouth what the answer was – before they sent Peter home. Before they finished patching Jonah up and driving him away. Before Mom came to take me back, or else I got sent to foster care.

He went right up to the window and looked down at the lake, almost pressing his face against the glass. He was only a few feet away, but he held his body awkwardly, like he didn't want to get too close to me. Was something the matter? My heart pounded again

– I felt that horrible taste in the back of my throat.

Maybe he'd seen me in the living room with Kyle. Maybe he'd been watching before he came in, so he knew what Kyle had tried to do. Maybe he was disgusted – it must have been pretty gross, Kyle tugging at my clothes like that, putting his hands all over me.

Or maybe he saw what I'd done. Maybe he'd counted along – one, two, three, four – while I bashed the butt of the gun down, again and again, on the top of Kyle's head.

Maybe he thought I was really messed up.

No, I thought. This is Peter – your friend.

He yawned, stretched out his arms, brushed the side of my shoulder with the tips of his fingers, touched them for a second, before letting them drop down again.

See?

I'd have to tell him what happened. I *wanted* to tell him – the whole story, even the nasty parts, so he'd know the truth.

When I turned to look at him, he was staring out the darkening window, his eyes wet, his mouth turned down, like his heart was breaking in two. He cleared his throat, wiped his eyes with the sleeve of his T-shirt.

'Etta,' he said.

I'd tell him about Kyle later. Now wasn't the time.

He was quiet for a few seconds, and that silence scared me. What was it he couldn't say?

In the end, it didn't matter. We stood side by side – not talking, not touching.

Between the high curtain of oak trees, I could just make out a scattering of silver stars. Below them, Yellow Lake glowed like a tarnished antique mirror.

Finally, Peter moved a little closer to me.

'It's still beautiful, isn't it?' he said. 'No matter what?'

I let out a deep sigh.

'Yeah,' I said. 'No matter what.'

JONAH

The heartbeat monitor was beeping crazily again. The paramedic hopped into the ambulance.

'Come on, Jonah, you know what to do.'

Jonah had no choice but to obey. He could barely speak, so he couldn't argue. He closed his eyes, slowed his breathing right down. He imagined the lake, a sunrise, a birch bark canoe. He saw another crazy vision. The two of them – him and Etta – paddling together, gliding silently into the light.

'There now. That's better.'

If only Etta could see it too.

Their time was almost up. The other ambulances had gone. All they were waiting for now was the chopper – his chopper, the one that would take him away.

Too soon, he thought, too soon. He panicked again, heard those staccato beeps.

Close your eyes. Think of Yellow Lake. Calm. Clear. Blue. Shiny smooth.

'Hi, Jonah.'

Etta stood outside the ambulance, looking in, waving an injured hand. The last low rays of the setting sun streamed in behind her, lighting her hair, reminding him of the first time she'd crawled clumsily into the wigwam. He closed his eyes, remembering.

'Is it OK to go in?'

The paramedic jumped back to the ground so that Etta could clamber up and sit on the floor beside his bed. She held out her hand to him – it was tiny inside his, soft, a little damp. He ran his fingers over her hers, explored with his thumb the ragged edges of her chewed nails, smoothed the broken, stitched-together skin.

Jonah felt tears coming on, a light trickle he couldn't quite blink back. He could blame the drugs later, if he wanted, he could blame the disorientation of being strapped to a gurney and tied up with tubing.

No. He had to stop this. He had to speak.

'I'm sorry,' he said. 'The wigwam. Leaving you.'

Etta shook her head. 'None of that matters any more, does it?'

The tears came again. Why didn't she get it? It *did* matter. He needed to start all over – build another wigwam, set new traps and snares, find that arrowhead he'd tossed away in anger and do some real fishing as he was meant to, with spears. He wanted to do it all again, the right way.

With her.

She squeezed his hand tightly. 'I saw what you did,' she said. 'You didn't have to let them do that.' She looked away from him, out the ambulance door, as if she could see something in the far distance.

'That was the hardest part,' she said. 'Watching you die.'

'Only I *didn't* die,' he wanted to say. 'Only I'm *not* dead. And I want to stay here, only nobody will listen.' He blinked, groaned again, shook his head with as much passion as his cotton-wrapped brain would let him.

'Don't worry,' Etta said. 'It'll all be over in a little while.'

Over? He twisted on the stretcher, tried to pull off his mask.

Beep-beep-beep-beep-beep.

'No,' he shouted. At least, he thought he was shouting. 'Drive away.'

'What?' Etta leaned in more closely. Could she even hear him?

'Drive away. Let's go. You. Me. Peter, if he wants to. In this thing.'

It would be a long time before he learned whether or not he'd been making any sense. In his mind, he was telling Etta to steal the ambulance and drive them to a place where they could start a new life, together, without any adults to mess things up, just the three of them, living like brothers and sister, or boyfriend and girlfriend – she could take up with Peter, he didn't care, just as long as they were together, as long as they stayed. But everything was so hazy. Was he actually talking, or just dreaming again?

It was impossible to know for sure. Etta let go of his hand. Her face faded from his vision. His thoughts got lost in a shroud of incoherence and his voice was smothered by the noisy pillow that was an approaching helicopter circling overhead, looking for a safe place to land.

PETER

Out over the lake, a pale sliver of moon was rising.

They stood on the beach, just the two of them.

It was quiet. No more shouting of orders, no more sirens blaring or chopper blades whining. There was just the lapping of the lake, the whoosh of the trees.

Peter should have been happy. This was what he wanted, to be alone with her. But what was the point if he was going to lose her so soon, if what they'd gone through together – the fear, the pain, all the feelings they had, good or bad – counted for nothing?

The sweet-spice aroma rose from the ashes of Jonah's wigwam pyre. Peter poked at the embers with a stick, churning up the smell, making it stronger.

'What *is* that?' Etta asked

'What?'

'The smell. Some kind of incense?'

'Dunno, but it's lovely.'

Such an English word – lovely. He'd never thought

about it before, but now every sound he uttered made him feel like a stranger again.

'Lovely,' Etta said. 'I like that word.'

With that, she slipped her arm around his, encircling it slowly, before taking his hand. He squeezed it tightly, wanting its soft imprint to stay embedded on his palm forever. He closed his eyes, breathed in deeply, trying to memorize the smell, the feel of her hand, the closeness of her body – the sweetness of these final moments with her.

Out on the lake, a fish jumped. Up on the hill, a car door slammed.

Somebody had arrived at the cabin, somebody who would soon be down on the beach, prizing Etta away from him, taking her home.

It could have been the fire, and that mojo stuff Jonah put in to make it mystical. It could have been that he knew that Etta would be leaving soon and this would be his only chance. It could have been because he needed to taste something *good*, to feel something tender.

He took a deep breath of the cool, scented air. Something, *someone* perhaps, was giving him courage. He touched Etta's hair and looked into her beautiful blue eyes. Then he kissed her on the lips, and even though the sand was soft and uneven, he didn't trip over, or tremble, or do anything awkward. He kissed her for a long time and when he stopped so he could take a breath, Etta looked up at him, smiling, and said, 'Lovely.'

There should be fireworks, Peter thought, like Bonfire Night, like the Fourth of July.

Instead, they got another jumping fish – it was a bigger fish this time, though, and it made a louder splash. And as he and Etta stayed together, the night got darker, the air got clearer. The stars seemed brighter against the blackness. They flamed and flashed – just for the two of them, it seemed – like tiny, distant sparklers.

Chapter Fifteen
—
ETTA

Sometimes I wonder if I'll ever be the same. Mom wonders, too.

She looks at me – while I'm watching TV or doing my homework at the kitchen table – and I know she's thinking, what really happened during those three days?

She'll turn her eyes away when I catch her at it, or else she'll smile and say something like, 'You look so pretty in that light.' But I know what's really on her mind.

She had all kinds of questions at the beginning. 'What did that bastard do to you? Did he touch you anywhere, you know, anywhere funny?'

Like that was all that mattered. Not thinking I was about to get shot. Not watching Jonah nearly die, or thinking Peter was already dead. Not almost bashing somebody's brains in.

'He barely touched me, Mom.'

'*Barely?*' she shrieked. 'What does that mean? *Barely?*'

I had questions for her, too – ones I never asked. 'How could you let that man get near me?' 'How come you couldn't even protect your own kid?'

When she came to pick me up at the cabin that night she wasn't wearing a low-cut top or skintight jeans. She was dressed in a knee-length black skirt and a white polyester blouse that wasn't even see-through. It was like she was on trial, standing in front of a judge, and maybe she was. She had to look like a real mom, act like a real mom, talk like a real mom, for the first time in her life.

Then, as soon as she saw me, wrapped up in a silver blanket left behind by the paramedics, she ran across the lawn to where I was waiting.

'My baby, my baby,' she screamed, like a hysterical kid.

I couldn't move. I had to wait there, completely still, while she slobbered all over me with her wet kisses and tears. I wanted to tell her I wasn't her baby, I wasn't her *anything*, I was me now, I was Etta, and being related to her was just a random accident.

That's what I felt, at least that's what I *thought* I was feeling, until she finally stopped shrieking and opened her arms. I let her hug me, and that was it.

Mom was Mom again. I was her girl, at least for a while.

So it was back to the trailer park for her and me. The night we got home she told me she never believed any of the crap Kyle told her about me. 'Not one word of it,' she bragged. 'Not for one second.' Like that was some big achievement. She said she would've called the cops, too – 'straight away, no waiting' – except that lying s.o.b. had told her that Grandpa had come by and picked me up.

'I ain't making excuses,' she said.

But she was. I knew it. She did, too.

Lucky for her, those excuses were good enough for the FBI. They searched the trailer and found some amphetamine traces, so they hauled her to St Paul for questioning. How much did she know about what Kyle was doing? Moving up from Minnesota – what was that all about? 'That's some track record with criminals, lady – don't you think?'

The lawyers told her she was lucky not to have gone to jail, lucky not to have had me put into foster care. They said she was lucky the cops believed what I told them – Mom was at work that night, there was no way she could've known that Kyle wasn't making auto parts or toilet paper or whatever he said he did.

But the worst thing about being back at the trailer didn't have anything to do with Kyle or Mom or the FBI. Missing Peter and Jonah – that was the toughest part. They were the only people I wanted to be with, the ones I knew I could trust. I texted Jonah and sent messages to Peter, but that made me feel even lonelier, somehow. It was like being in prison, talking that way. All those words without faces, those feelings without touch.

Sometimes I felt bad about being so miserable. I should have been grateful – we were all alive, weren't we? We were in our homes, safe with our families. Everything was back to normal, the way it was before.

That's what I told myself, but I knew it wasn't true.

It wasn't back to normal, at least not for me.

PETER

Everything was too noisy when he got back to England.

Heathrow was a nightmare, the screeching crowds of people and the shrill tannoy announcements. He had to run to the toilet again, shivering and sick, and wait with the door locked until his heart stopped pounding.

You're not dying, he told himself, you're not dying, you're not dying, you're not dying – not fucking *now*.

Delayed shock, the doctor told him, like a post-traumatic stress reaction. 'You've had a tough time, I hear,' he said, his hand on Peter's shoulder, squeezing it with each syllable.

A tough time. Yeah, just a little.

His father had gone all caring and sharing, too. 'Are you too cold, son? Should I put on the heating?' The constant referral to what had happened at the cabin – 'You can talk to me, you know, whenever you want.

Or a counsellor? Would that be better?' – made him almost miss the days when Dad had seemed like an arrogant git.

Almost, but not quite. This new-model Dad was all right, actually. He brought Peter cups of tea, made him bacon butties. He took care of him – a proper father.

What really hurt was missing Etta. And Jonah, too, funnily enough. The messages from America helped, but the effect only lasted for a few minutes. They were too chatty and insubstantial, so flimsy and transparent, that there was no point reading them more than once. The real Etta and the real Jonah were somewhere else, not online – in an actual place, far, far away.

When summer came, he could go back to Yellow Lake – Dad had promised. Until then, he'd have to go through the motions – get ready for his GCSEs, watch football on the TV, take the train to London on weekends, do the usual things, Camden market with some mates, maybe a gig at the Forum or the Brixton Academy.

Walking around the streets of London, pushing his way onto buses and storming down the escalators for the Tube, he remembered how terrified he used to be in the city – what if he got attacked by a gang of youths? What if he lost his railcard or got off at the wrong stop?

He'd catch a glimpse of himself in the Tube train window now, and he'd think how odd it was that he looked the same. Dyed blond, sticky-out hair, blue eyes, tatty jeans, polo shirt, high-tops. Like any other white kid, up from Sussex for the day, anxious about knife crime and bombings and missing the last train home.

The train would shudder to a sudden stop and the other passengers would gasp and struggle to stay on their feet. He'd see their anxious looks – what was *that*? But he'd just tighten his grip on the handrail, plant his feet more firmly on the floor. He wasn't scared.

Not any more.

JONAH

The operation to remove the bullet had been so simple. The surgeons had made a tiny cut in his shoulder and picked the bullet out with something that looked like giant tweezers. It was as if the whole experience of being shot, of feeling – no, *knowing* – that he was going to die wasn't any worse than getting a splinter. He was home in a couple of days, his arm in a sling, his tiny wound covered with an overgrown Band-Aid that had to be changed every so often.

For the first few days, his mother had just cried.

Later, during the second week, she started to talk, and, for Jonah, that was worse. When she was just crying, he didn't have to do anything, just pat her on the shoulder occasionally, or give her a hug, let her cling onto him for a few minutes like he was some kind of life raft. But once she started talking again, he was expected to answer.

'Why did you run away?' she'd bawl.

When he tried to tell her that he didn't run *away*, but *towards* something else, towards a part of himself that he still needed to find, it was as if she couldn't hear him.

'Was I such a bad mom?'

He'd sigh and try again. 'I just needed to be by myself for a while. Find a place of my own, live the way I was meant to.'

'But why?' Her face would crumple and turn red. 'Was being shot by drug dealers better than being stuck here with *me*?'

Sometimes, when he couldn't take any more, he'd stomp out of the apartment, and slip down the back stairs to the alley that cut through to Lake Street.

Lake Street was like a battle zone – torn-up sidewalks, jackhammers blasting like heavy artillery, everybody on foot being shunted past barricades, like refugees. Most of them were Latinos who'd traded poverty in Mexico for hard work and long hours up north. Some were Somalis, driven out of their home country by war and starvation. All of them – Jonah and his mom, too, most likely – would soon be on the move again. Once the roads were rebuilt, once the derelict buildings were turned into expensive condos for rich hipsters, the whole community would be scattered again, forced to scramble around looking for cheaper places to live.

On one of these walks, Jonah passed a trendy coffee place that had just opened up on the corner where there used to be a dry-cleaners and a shoe repairer. There weren't any Latinos or Somalis inside, drinking skinny decaf lattes, though. And the people at the serving counters were all whiter than he was.

How funny was that? All the time he'd wanted to escape the white man's world. He'd never realized that the Lake Street he grew up in – with the little grocery stores, the Mexican cafés, the cheap hardware stores selling bags of nails for fifty cents – wasn't part of the white world either. Pretty soon, though, it would be, and now it was too late to change it.

It got cold after a few minutes. The air felt sharp and tingly in his nostrils – it would snow pretty soon. On his way back home he bought a $1.59 box of Hot Tamales candy for his mother. Then he stopped at the cheap hardware store and bought a red self-stick gift bow for a quarter.

It was nearly dark when he climbed back up the stairs. The smell of spaghetti sauce in the kitchen – tomatoes and garlic, basil and onions – made him realize that he was starving, and reminded him of how hungry he'd been, living on his own in the wigwam. He put his arms around his mom's slender shoulders. She took his present, laughed for a second before crying again.

Later, when they'd finished eating, she talked about her father. The anniversary of his death had occurred while Jonah was at Yellow Lake. She'd gone to the veterans' cemetery at Fort Snelling and laid a wreath on his grave for the first time in years. Something about Jonah being gone made her feel lonesome – even the dead could be company, she guessed. And at the cemetery, something weird came over her. Maybe it was all the waving flags, all the patriotic slogans, but when she read her dad's name – PFC Norman Grove, US Army, 1969-70, 4th Battalion, Light Infantry – she felt proud. Her dad had fought for his country. Whatever he did later, however he messed up the rest of his life, he was a *hero*, he was buried in a hero's grave.

And while she was driving back home over the Mendota bridge, a *really* freaky thing had happened – a bald eagle flew across the river. It soared upstream then swooped down under the bridge. She'd never seen an eagle before, not in the Cities.

She got so excited she nearly crashed the car.

'S'pose you think that's some kind of sign,' she said, smiling. 'Some kind of big Indian deal.'

Jonah shrugged. 'Dunno.'

She smiled again, tears filling her eyes. 'It *was*, wasn't it? Some Ojibwe deal.'

After he had cleared their plates away, she talked about how much she'd missed him while he was gone, how she'd almost gone crazy with worry. He was the only family she had left – that was the important thing – and she never wanted to lose him.

'This other stuff,' she said, waving her hands, 'the running away, the getting hurt, that little girl – pretty soon you won't even remember. You'll forget all about what happened one of these days.'

His mother leaned over the table and held his face in her trembling hands.

He closed his eyes. 'You're probably right, Mom.'

But under his sweater and T-shirt, the star-shaped scar on his shoulder itched – a sign, Jonah knew it. He wasn't going to forget about what happened at Yellow Lake. Not today. Not tomorrow.

His mother kissed his forehead and sat back down.

Jonah opened his eyes and smiled at her.

Never.

ETTA

They said on the weather that there'd be a snowstorm over the weekend, the first big fall of the winter, so everybody driving over the Thanksgiving holiday should be extra careful.

We weren't driving anywhere. Mom refused to budge, even though we'd been invited down to Grandpa and Grandma's. (The Duchess had been so nice after what happened – phone calls and presents, thoughtful little cards – I decided it was time to call her by her rightful title.) People could come to her if they wanted, Mom said. Sure, she lived in a pokey trailer, but that didn't mean she couldn't cook for a big crowd.

So, Thanksgiving morning, I told her I was going back to Yellow Lake before the snow covered it all up.

'Are you crazy?' Mom squawked, in her usual my-way-or-the-highway voice. 'It's Thanksgiving. Company's coming.'

I told her maybe I was crazy and that I'd go anyway, no matter what she said. I didn't care, I told her. I'd walk, I'd hitchhike. I'd steal a car if I had to.

After that, she didn't put up a fight. She turned the oven down on the turkey, put her coat on, grabbed her purse.

'OK, then, honey, I'll take you. Now. Tomorrow. Whenever you want.' She said it seriously, like she meant it, like she understood how important it was.

We took the exact route Kyle had taken the night I jumped out of the car – past the IGA store, turning at the stop sign by the boarded up drive-in, then down the highway that had the blacktop ripped off and was still only gravel.

I was getting sweaty. It was freezing cold outside, but I had to roll down the window, let in some air. I looked outside, watched the trees go by, gray and bare now – the same trees that had flashed by me that night in the dark.

The cabin wasn't the same, though, with Mom along. It was just a place, one I hardly recognized. When we pulled into the driveway I could still see the tracks made by all the cars and the ambulances that tore up the lawn. Mom turned off the engine and I looked out my window. There were cigarette butts on the ground, a few burnt matches and a drop of something that looked like blood – a dark red stain on the brittle leaves.

We got out of the car. The cabin was boarded up, so I couldn't see inside. Mom followed me across the lawn, around the side of the house, like she was scared to let me out of her sight. She kept asking me things, like how far in the woods did Kyle take those Mexican guys and where was that window you climbed out of and why didn't you just call home so we could come and get you?

She was like a yappy terrier with a bone – she wouldn't let up. Or maybe she couldn't. Maybe she *had* to know about these things to reassure herself that nothing *really* bad happened and that I would be OK in the end – that *we'd* be OK.

Finally, I asked her to wait in the car. She looked hurt at first, her eyes big and watery. Then her hurt gave way to a flicker of anger. I could tell she wanted to snap something back at me, like, 'Don't tell me what to do, little girl,' but she didn't. It was like the fight was drained out of her now. She looked pale and fragile. A strong wind could have just blown her away.

She started toward the car, shoulders hunched, but

then she stopped and turned around again. 'Etta?'

'Now what?' I said.

Her face was scrunched up and she wiped her eyes with the sleeve of her coat.

'I wish I'd never stopped looking for you,' she said. 'I wish I'd found you. I wish I'd. . .'

She was crying now, big fat tears rolling down her face.

'It was all my fault.' She choked and sobbed. 'I know that now.'

I should have gone to her and put my arms around her. I should have said, 'No, Mom, of course it wasn't. It was just one of those things. An accident, Mom.'

But I didn't want to lie any more, not about anything.

Especially not here.

She slunk back to the car. I went to the side of the cabin where the wigwam had been. There was no sign of it now, no flattened grass or brush, no leftover traces of Jonah's painted bark strips. In only a few months it had all sprung back to the wild. There was no sign of Peter's path to the Nussbaums's either. Nothing of us had been left behind. So what if the snow covered it up like a blanket?

The lake would be better. I stumbled down the

hill, almost tumbling into the water when my legs hit the soft sand. The wind cut right through me. Waves rose up in the steel-gray water like shards of white-tipped metal. Jonah's fire was still there on the beach, though. The fragrant ashes had blown away, some of the stones were covered up by shifting sand, but it didn't matter. Like his patch of blood on the lawn, Jonah's fire had left behind a dark, lasting scar.

I sat next to the stone circle, cross-legged, and let the cold seep through the seat of my jeans. The wind rifled its icy fingers through the gaps in my jacket where the buttons were gone, but I didn't care – the cold and the wind were like company here. I picked up a fallen twig and drew random, thoughtless circles on the sand. If only I could stay here till summer, like this, a frozen statue, hibernating until Jonah and Peter came back.

The twig hit a rock and started to shake. Was it something to do with the fire, some leftover crazy stuff that Jonah had put on it to make it smell strong? No. The fire had been out for months, there wasn't any smell – the only thing making the twig shake were my frozen, soon-to-be-frostbitten fingers.

In a few weeks the lake would start to freeze over. In a month or two there'd be snowmobiles instead of waterskiers, ice-fishing huts instead of motorboats. Nothing could survive out here in the winter, not even Jonah's magic.

Up on the hilltop, Mom honked the horn.

It was time to do what I had to do.

I reached into the pocket of my jeans and took out the tiny velvet bag that contained Peter's precious treasure. I pulled open the little drawstring cord to check and make sure it was still inside.

The hair looked frizzy and matted, but it was still a shiny auburn, like he said it would be. I pulled the string as tight as I could, to keep out the cold. And where the twig was, I dug a hole with my bare fingers – under the dry sand, into the wet and harder dirt underneath.

I placed the velvet bag in the hole and covered it up again. I pushed in the twig, forked side up, and built a little mound around it with rocks and stones.

It didn't seem like much of a memorial. There was nothing for me to write on, nothing for me to write with. By spring it wouldn't even be here, but maybe that was the point.

I said a prayer, or the closest thing I could come up with.

Take care of this lady, wherever she is.

Take care of her son, his friends – Jonah and me.

The horn went again.

Take care of Mom, too. Especially her.

On my way back up the hill the snow started, tiny flecks that glowed against the gray sky like electrified dust. I turned around when I got to the top, took one last look. Even now, with only the tiniest specks of snow in the air, it looked different. It reminded me of what Peter had written after he got back to England, about *his* last look.

It was so different from the plane, he'd said. There were so many lakes on the ground, hundreds of them, not just one. He'd squinted out the window, tried to see things, recognize landmarks – the path through the woods, the line on the beach where the woods joined it, the circle of stones on the beach where Jonah had burned the wigwam.

There was nothing – just dozens of dark, formless spots. But he had felt something, even from high in the ice-cold air – a pull, like the tide.

When I got home that Thanksgiving I pulled out the copy I had made of his letter. He always could say things better than me:

Perhaps a place can draw you to it, Etta, the way people

can. Yellow Lake must have had a global magnetic pull, don't you think? When worlds collide and all that? But was what happened to you and me and Jonah just a collision, Etta? Did we bounce off each other and then get flung back out into the orbit of empty space, like tiny chunks of broken planet?

Or did we fuse? Bond, invisibly, to form a new, more powerful body?

I know what I think, he said.

I know what I think, too.

Read more about *At Yellow Lake* at
www.atyellowlake.co.uk
You can visit Jane's blog at
janemcloughlin.blogspot.com
and follow her on Twitter @JBMcloughlin.

JANE MCLOUGHLIN is originally from the USA
but has lived in the UK for over twenty years.
She's written screenplays, radio dramas and had
several short stories published. Jane lives in Brighton
with her husband and two children,
and teaches English in a secondary school.
At Yellow Lake is her debut novel.

Acknowledgments

I owe so much to the following people: the staff of Cornerstones Literary Consultancy, particularly Helen Corner; Sara O'Connor and Sara Grant, who edited Undiscovered Voices 2010; everyone at Frances Lincoln Children's Books, especially the wonderful Maurice Lyon and my brilliant editor, Emily Sharratt.

Thanks, too, to early readers and supporters: Patsy Fergusson, Jordan Benson, Kay Syrad, Clare Leech, Wendy Griggs, Sarah Wheddon and Liz Lee.

In July, 2011, my family's actual cabin was damaged in a terrifying and catastrophic windstorm. The following people offered much help: Marcia Holmberg, Dan Seemon, Wayne Holmberg, Marilyn Boe, Don and Sherry Ladig, Merriam Park Neighbors for Peace members including Pop, Thea, Margie, Margret, Beth, Joe, Tim, Suzanne, Tivey and Krista. Thanks, too, to the professionals, especially Ryan, Buba, Rob and Terry.

Special thanks go to Mark Benson, my brother; Anne Benson, my sister; and to Peggy Benson and Jim Dixon.

To my son Sean and daughter Hannah – thanks for your encouragement, your enthusiasm, and for making me laugh!

To my husband Jim – thanks for believing, even when I didn't.

Finally, posthumous thanks to Hildegarde Wright, a dear writer and friend; and to Eileen O'Neill, who I miss every day.

Note

At Yellow Lake is a work of fiction. Although some place names are real, the settings I've written about do not always resemble the actual location.

I'd also like to point out that, in reality, Jonah would have had access to many Native American cultural and educational organisations within and around the Twin Cities of Minneapolis and St Paul.

For more information on Ojibwe language and culture, a good starting place is the website www.Ojibwe.net.